BENDING HOME

Selected & New Poems
1967–1998

Bending Home

SELECTED & NEW POEMS
1967–1998

Susan Griffin

COPPER CANYON PRESS
Port Townsend, Washington

Cover art: Morris Graves's *April Flowering Cabbage and a Glimpse of Continuing*. 1995, acrylic on paper, 31 × 44 inches.

Printed in the United States of America.

The publication of this book was supported by grants from the Lannan Foundation, the National Endowment for the Arts, the Washington State Arts Commission, and by contributions from Elliott Bay Book Company, James Laughlin, and the members of the Friends of Copper Canyon Press. Copper Canyon Press is in residence with Centrum at Fort Worden State Park.

Copper Canyon Press would also like to thank Morris Graves and the Schmidt-Bingham Gallery for the permission to reprint *April Flowering Cabbage and a Glimpse of Continuing*.

Library of Congress Cataloging-in-Publication Data

Griffin, Susan.
Bending home: selected and new poems / by Susan Griffin.
p. cm.

ISBN 1-55659-087-3
I. Title.
PS3557.R48913 B46 1998
811'.54 – DDC21   98-19743
                                                              CIP

9 8 7 6 5 4 3 2 FIRST EDITION

COPPER CANYON PRESS
P.O. Box 271
Port Townsend, WA 98368

ACKNOWLEDGMENTS

Some of the poems in this collection previously appeared in *Like the Iris of an Eye* (Harper and Row, 1976) and *Unremembered Country* (Copper Canyon Press, 1987).

Grateful acknowledgment is made to the publishers of the following books and magazines in which some of the poems have appeared:

Aldebaran Review; *Amazon Quarterly*; *Amazon Poetry* (Out and Out Books); *Anthology of Women Poets* (Dremen); *Big Moon*; *Breadloaf Quarterly*; *Countrywomen*; *Dear Sky* (Shameless Hussy Press); *Everywoman*; *From Shadows Emerging*; *It Ain't Me, Babe*; *Kyoto Review*; *Lesbian Reader* (Amazon Press); *Let Them Be Said* (Mama's Press); *Made From This Earth*; *Mosaic*; *Mountain Moving Day* (The Crossing Press); *Ms.*; *New*; *New England Review*; *The New Women's Survival Sourcebook* (Alfred A. Knopf and Co.); *Nineteen New American Poets of the Golden Gate*; *No More Masks* (Doubleday and Co.); *Peace or Perish, a Crisis Anthology*; *Rising Tides* (Washington Square Press); *Plexus*; *Room*; *Shocks*; *This is Women's Work* (Panjandram Press); *War Resisters Calendar*; *What Woman, and Who, Myself, I Am* (Wooden Shoe Press); *Woman Poet, Volume 1: The West*.

"Summer Night" has been set to music by Albert Greenberg and arranged by Bob Davis for a work in progress performed by a traveling Jewish theater in collaboration with Joseph Chaikin and Mira Rafalowicz.

"Knowledge of the Body" has been set to music by Suzanne Vicenza and arranged as a jazz suite by *Alive*. "Born into a World Knowing" and "Summer Night" appear in *What Book? Buddha Poems from Beat to Hip Hop* (Parallax Press); "Prayer for Continuation" appears in *Atomic Ghosts* (Coffee House Press); "Our Mother" appears in *Claiming the Spirit Within* (Beacon Press); "Teeth," "Stories and Poems," and "Miracle" appear in *Cries of the Spirit* (Beacon Press); "She Tries to Reason it Out" appears in *Waste Land: Meditations on a Ravaged Landscape* (Aperture).

The poems from "Letter" first appeared in a handset book, entitled *Letter* and published by Effie's Press. "Thicket" was published in its entirety by *The Kenyon Review*; "To the Far Corners of a Fractured World" appeared in *A Gift of Tongues*; "Curve" was first published by the *Nuclear Guardianship Forum* and "Home" appeared in *Inquiring Mind*.

I would also like to thank Anita Barrows who read this collection with great sensitivity, my editors Sam Hamill and Michael Wiegers for their patient and enthusiastic support of this volume, and my deep gratitude to Morris Graves for allowing me to use his extraordinary work on the cover of this book.

– Susan Griffin
July 1998

CONTENTS

VII

This book is lovingly dedicated
to my daughter,
Chloe Andrews,
and to her daughter,
Sophie Liberty Andrews

☘ ☘ ☘

BENDING HOME

Selected & New Poems
1967–1998

THE WOMAN

The woman
with teeth like a horse
moves swiftly
her jaw silhouetted against
life the carriage, a
passing
green curve
the fall bushes
shiver in the
mild white sun, a face
passing over the face of the earth,
a young colt
is reflected in her teeth
his tendons gleaming we are
growing old
and hold
each smell inside
and see the sky through
the smell of your sperm
and our sweat, one could die
to look at your long
irregular toes
we sitting on the ground
your hand
in the wetness
between my arm and my
breast, the wet, the
bush, your white shirt
smiles at me

saying this is a
moment, now, right now
a terrible moment
a colt is being born
in my mind covered with
his mother's blood
she licks off
in my skull
the old horse
hooves sticky
limps among weeds
your shirt
smiles at me
and I feel
my heart
pumping
blood
turning
my face red.

1967

CONSUMMATION

I wake with the word
in my mind, *Consummation*,
the muscular valley, the harvest
so high it begins to cascade,
petals stretching themselves like
old breasts, skin of thinness like
veils, like a blouse soaked
in sweat, smeared with the yellow
powder of fingertips, fused
full with a sky that reaches
brazenly, all the way down,
unashamedly deep to the ground.
This is the nature of depth,
the black tip far inside
the petal, the place within
that widens a mouth to drink.

1984

BREAD

They baked bread and put
everything in it,
you said.
I picture you in a
loaf of bread
they have shaped
around you.
They lay with their
bodies unclothed together.
So beautiful, you said.
Flesh to flesh
to bread I keep
this in my mind.
It makes my day sweet.

1971

REVOLUTION

I would not have gotten in this boat with you.
I would not
except
where else was there
at the dock's end
to go?
The water
was cold.

I would not have let you row the boat.
I could see
what kind of man you were.
I would not but
who was there to choose
between
you and me?

I would not have let you throw away the oars.
I knew what would happen next,
except
what else was there to do,
struggle
in a boat with a leak
over cold water?

1970

SHE WAS TWENTY-THREE

I was nineteen,
she had slashed her wrists
and tried other things.
She was blond and thin, and
wandered about places
looking at the floor.
I had known her husband, and
I had seen her once before,
before the wrists.
She was bright and quick then,
still I liked her better
after. I met her once
in a hallway moving
from apartment to apartment
and have not seen her since.
I need to know now
is she still
alive and
how?

1970

HER SADNESS RUNS
BESIDE HER LIKE A HORSE

Her sadness runs beside her
like a horse
    now she is
riding the horse of her sadness
  riding, riding, riding.
Does she wear a hat?
No.
That is her hair you see
which the wind
whips into her eyes.
Does she cry?
No.
The wind cries
the horse cries
she grips his body
with her thighs,
they are changing
direction
riding into the sun.
Who
knows the way,
the woman or the
horse-of-her-sadness?
Her thighs know
his body knows.
Will they ever stop
riding?
What?
Look,

now they have
traveled
below the horizon.
Now we can
only wait.
Will they
ever
return?
But they are
here now.
Where?
Listen,
don't you hear
them
galloping
under this earth?

1972

LOVE SHOULD GROW UP LIKE
A WILD IRIS IN THE FIELDS

Love should grow up like a wild iris in the fields,
unexpected, after a terrible storm, opening a purple
mouth to the rain, with not a thought to the future,
ignorant of the grass and the graveyard of leaves
around, forgetting its own beginning. Love should
grow like a wild iris
but does not.
Love more often is to be found in kitchens at the dinner hour,
tired out and hungry, lingers over tables in houses where
the walls record movements; while the cook is probably angry,
and the ingredients of the meal are budgeted, while
a child cries feed me now and her mother not quite
hysterical says over and over, wait just a bit, just a bit,
love should grow up in the fields like a wild iris
but never does
really startle anyone, was to be expected, was to be
predicted, is almost absurd, goes on from day to day, not quite
blindly, gets taken to the cleaners every fall, sings old
songs over and over, and falls on the same piece of rug that
never gets tacked down, gives up, wants to hide, is not
brave, knows too much, is not like an
iris growing wild but more like
staring into space
in the street
not quite sure
which door it was, annoyed about the sidewalk being
slippery, trying all the doors, thinking
if love wished the world to be well, it would be well.
Love should

grow up like a wild iris, but doesn't, it comes from
the midst of everything else, sees like the iris
of an eye, when the light is right,
feels in blindness and when there is nothing else is
tender, blinks, and opens
face up to the skies.

1972

GRENADINE

The movies, she told me
ruined my life.
We were sitting there
drinking bourbon and soda
flavored by grenadine.
I in the leather chair
that engulfed me
carrying me back,
on the television
a late movie
we weren't watching,
its noise took up our silences.
She was fat from all her drinking
and her eyes darted
unfocused about the room
her voice jumped from deep
to high laughter.
Really, she said,
No kidding, she said,
I mean that. The
movies, she said,
curling her lip
and looking meanly
at George Sanders
on the TV.
They, she said,
pointing and accusing,
tell you things about life
that aren't true.

She sat
staring a long time
trying to focus on my eyes.
Hello, Sweetie, she said
and smiled at me
like a cockeyed white hula
dancer from inside a plastic
ukulele. She put her glass embellished with
splashes of gold on the metal TV tray
her feet on the leather stool.
She had it fixed
so she never had to move.
Your father, she said,
he was a good man,
do you know why
we di-
vorced?
"No."
I stared at the
grenadine in my bourbon.
Because of the movies,
she said.
I blinked past her eyes
heaved in the leather chair
trying to upright myself
trying to refill my glass,
the television
busily selling cars,
my stepfather snoring on

the couch
like a giant vacuum cleaner.
She laughed
a high-pitched laugh and tried
her very best
to stare right at me.
We would go to the movies
your father and I.
I nodded at her.
And I'd come out
being Carole Lombard,
only he refused
to be Humphrey Bogart.
We stared at each other,
the television
sticking to the sides of our faces
George Sanders pretending to be
evil pretending to be good
being unmasked by
Rosalind Russell pretending
to be a lady reporter
pretending in real life
all she really wanted was
a home and family she said
to *Ladies' Home Journal* reporter but
job of acting and stardom
thrust upon her
never found right man.
All the myths, my mother

said. *I saw a movie*
about, about
they made me think, she said,
running off with another man
would be African jungle
beautiful in dark green
Don Ameche canoeing to
palace in wilderness
speaking mad poetry
of love
absolute lusty
freedomofitall
glorious spirit of man
kissing
in white bow tie
and unconquerable
white orchid
maraschino cherry red lips
she said
they made it look so glamorous
drinking her grenadine bourbon
and fell asleep,
my stepfather snoring
on the couch
while the dog
whined outside the screen door
to be let in.

1970

CINEMA REALITÉ

Scenes from a Childhood

I am in the classroom.
The other children
have all left,
the space ship is
departing, I
grab my pencil
and jump
on board.

We accelerate
but once outside
gravity, I fall,
Space is
sucking me
away!

How long
can the
body survive
out here,
no food,
no water,
Hold
onto me,
I cry.

Fantasia

We are at the table when
her parents come, they fly
through open windows
on small planes.
     Where's the sunshine?
they complain.
The sun obliges them.
     Sunshine! I realize while
her husband
goes to the kitchen for
two more plates.

Next, I am staring at her father.
He wears emeralds
in his crown and claps
his hands for service
from his wife
who is sugaring
phantom cups of coffee.
     I'm in love with
     your daughter,
I tell him quickly,
before her husband can
return with the
china.

The table is silent now
but as her husband returns
his wife, the daughter
begins to laugh,
then we begin to laugh together
and soon we nod and soon we stand,
announcing
      We are leaving.

Halfway to the door
she will stop
to see her father
set down his diadem
and begin to weep.
      I am no longer King.

Here, she may start to shake her
head in sympathy
but I will grab
an emerald
while the dinner party
collapses. Then while
centuries of crockery
crash through
the ceiling, as
we try to go
we are
nearly crushed by
a five hundred year

old table setting,
ancien régime.

But in this movie
     we survive
and on the street
figures dart
from every door.

Touring France

There are five.
As we drive
through the French
countryside.
Two of us
are lovers.
They stay
in a separate car,
heads like two dogs
groomed alike
close and sensitive to stray
sound.

We remark on how
well these heads
look together
both curly.

When we step out
they stare through us
as lovers do
interested only in
each other.

Because
I am not a lover

I wonder,
Where are we going?

The buildings begin to look alike too, stone
farmhouses, white town houses, gray city walls.
There are significant harbors and
migrating birds and waters that
cure illness, or
sequester poison fish who
attack young children.
The fifth traveler leaves us
in Vannes
purposefully neglecting
to say good-bye
to the lovers.
Now there are four
two a couple
and two not.

The lovers go by
a different road
stopping at a town
where Gauguin lived.

We who are left
and not a couple still
translate our lives
from French to English

to French, admiring
the countryside.

We meet at a crossing
speed back through darkness.
What am I doing?
I ask, *Why*
am I unhappy?

There is no possible lover
here.
Restless I take the morning
train. My friend's small
body diminishes
on the platform
while the lovers
await her
at a café.

Brittany speeds past
sending me messages.
What do you want?
A green blur of trees,
Why does there always
the light shines in
have to be a lover
fields rush by
do you want
small cows congregate

against a hill
to live on
a pond shimmers
in the body
darkness, a wall
of another?

I am the last of five
the last face on the screen.
And when someone
in the audience asks
What's this movie about?
I protest
Je ne parle pas Français.

Gendarmes

The French police come running
across the square
like water searching for
a level.
The French police all
look alike and are no bigger
than my thumb.
Each wears the habit
of a nun,
then a blue cape,
then nun again,
but they keep moving,
an urgent careen
from foot to foot
as if a key were turned
behind.
They know they must
arrest someone.
Their lives depend on crime
and there isn't time
enough for each
to succeed. Like ants
always a few must die.
Methodical and calm
they fan past
the gilded gates.
While in the prefecture

everyone is stamped
with a face,
only we who watch
feel fear.
But the screen is space
drenched with color
and this is what we have
bargained for.
This is why
we are here.

The Last of the French Movies

1

The images are paling now.
The camera draws away
leaves us without a screen.
The air
touches
everything.
We are dependent
on the weather
of our souls, no
image
covers us, our
terror
is wholly
real, our love the
thinnest thread
what we dread now
as familiar as dreams.
Everything is
what it seems.

2

In my dreams
escaping over ice
in the frozen tundra
I am embraced
by a polar bear
and though

I am terrified, this
bear looks on me tenderly as
I fall in love
for an instant.

3

The polar bear embraces me
Cold water embraces me
My bones become ice
My flesh is blue

4

I am not image
I am substance:

> when I sigh
> the frost of my breath
> leaves evidence:

I was here.

And to this lone
creature I see
passing, I whisper:

lick the ice
drink
know me.

1975

FALL

Fall down to the earth
the earth doesn't care
is cool is deep is dark is
curved into a red
sun going down is
burning at its edges, fall
into this earth
let this earth cover you.
Cover you in water,
in mud, dust,
grass, air,
in wind, let the
wind blow over you
and fall and lie gentle
on the sweet face,
spin
around the sun and through
the stars, the night
forget
the night and all
you know, close
your eyes and open your
mouth, suffocate and be swallowed,
be digested, become
shit in the fields and
seed to grow and bloom and fester
die and fall, fall,
fall.

1971

from LETTER

✼ ✼ ✼

the blackness
a refuge deeper
than sleep
your arm
mooring me
by the
waist.

∨ ∨ ∨

we started
under eucalyptus
rain wetting
our faces our eyes
startled shutters
taking the moments like
shocks, our hands
in pockets
resting bodies
side by side
the quick electric
body of a dog between
us springing
at each sound each
movement.

⚶ ⚶ ⚶

they were lost in
traffic
or had
forgotten the passport, or
missed the
scheduled time and
struggling to
get there
shouted at one
another all they
had kept back
for one long
year, the pain
like green wood
inside them.

⽵ ⽵ ⽵

I hoped to see
your truck
calmly there
on the street
and you calmly
inside lying
your eyes
half-closed on a book
under your falling
arm, turning
your body
to mine
as I slide
in the flowered sheets
your knees up
against my
ass.

✹ ✹ ✹

this is a letter written
to events,
why couldn't you
have been
different! This is
a letter to
circumstances,
my god why did
you have to be?
Don't
answer.
I've answered
and answered
and answered;
this is a letter to
me, my
letter
I keep reading
and then writing
and then reading
myself.

✷ ✷ ✷

I walk in the
rain holding my daughter's hand.
If I am sad
my sadness falls on her
                    like the rain.
What can I do?

Perversity

Oh I want to
tell you
how you have
hurt me,
to describe every
point of exquisite
pain and to
what end?
So you will
take me in
your arms and
then
let me
stroke your sweet hair.

1973

ARCHAEOLOGY OF A LOST WOMAN: FRAGMENTS

1

A book stained with
years of use:
The Joy of Cooking.

The pieces
of a mixing bowl
taken apart
displayed
by her granddaughter
as sculpture.

Her sweater, knitted
magenta wool.

Her hands, long
misshapen fingers spotted
brown.

The old needles
the old patterns.

Her voice still saying,
If my face is stern
it is because it has grown
to look that way
despite me.

2

A walk through a
museum, women
in photography, a
picture of
an ironing board, an
iron before a window,
a shadow cast in the
natural light.

3

She remembers holding her hand,
her grandmother's secret
knowledge,
the two boarding the trolley, the
yearly trip downtown,
the school clothes, the
joy that day, the
laughter between the two, the
promise of something sweet at
home, the old woman, her
promise.

She remembers longing
to walk
the light out there
beautiful
through the open door.

She remembers words
to her daughter, *Hurry,*
be
careful, don't
spill
over me. She remembers

her grandmother's voice
the hardness, then,
the weariness.

4

Words in an old diary
Sunday, March 23, 1958

Home all day. Black clouds. Quite
dark at times. However I did laundry
so I could go out in the morning. Dried
in and out. Quite a breeze. Washed doll
clothes. Must make her a footstool.
Finally made Ernie's fudge. Fried the
chicken in the pan and was moist
and very good. Rest and after went
to sleep. Bed at 9:30. Read a bit.
... Awake for ages. Too tired to get
up or read. Just tossed and turned...

5

In the museum
photographs of women
their hands over their mouths,

women standing
side by side
not touching
the lassitude of
unloving
in them,

etching of a woman alone
called *Waiting,*

woman and child
asleep in the railway station,

a face staring into the lens
I am what I am
broken, you will
see that in time.

a woman passed through
slavery, letting her eyes
blaze, *My body*
carries this pain
like an emblem.

I do not apologize.
I survive.

6

Child's memories
dolls cut
from cloth
new faces threaded
each year

candy distilled
to hardness
over the fire

an old drawing sent
through the mail,
I love you
Mommy.
Archaeology

the waters
of sleep we had
no time to swim.

My cries at night
the ache in my knees
her old stockings
around my legs

my daughter's nightmare
my arms around her, my
face pleading, *Don't*
wake up again.

Her tenderness, my desire to
please breaking like vases
along the lines of
an old fault,

the flower I gave her
she did not believe would bloom

ink spilled on the satin
bed covers, the furies
if you don't
welling inside her
stop crying
the darkness of my room
if you don't
stop

7

waters of sleep
flowers blooming
my daughter brought forward
like a sweet

My grandmother
floats in my dreams
we sleep

like sisters in
the peach-colored room
where I slept
as a child, and in
my womb I feed
the great-grandchild
she always wanted.

Archaeos, the
shards of
disbelief
the last words never
spoken how I
loved you old
complaining woman, the
pieces, the stairs
were slippery,
and she slipped,
broken one more
time,
pieces
her mixing bowl on my

the silver bell
she saved
for me.

8

Do you know
I ask her
calling through time
I write this
with your pen?

1976

MOTHER AND CHILD

Mother
I write home
I am alone and
give me my
body back.

(She drank
and drank and
did not feed me
I was the child at home.)

You have given me disease:
All
the old
areas of infection reopen themselves:
my breath
rasps,
my head
is an
argument,
my blood ebbs, you
and your damned Irish genes
did this to me.

I pretend
someone else
cares for me,
catches my
falling body,

cradles my
aching head,
cries when my fever rises
in alarm.

And meanwhile
Mother
from my dying bed
I have
finished you, you are
not even a
spot upon the sheet,
you are gamma-rayed
clean gone.

You are not
absent anymore
you
never were.

And your child
is the driven snow, she
is innocent of
all action, the
articulate say *victim,*
a word
she neither speaks nor
knows.

She is buried. She is only
bone, polished clean and white
as if with
agonized toil
a shrunken jeweler
crouched inside
her box
tumbling her body
by hand but
she was alone.

She was alone, but
her casket
was glass. And when she
cried she turned
her body
in shame
to the earth, and
turning and turning
wore her
body away.

Now
in my dreams
the mother who never was
finds the bones of her child
and says,
How we have both suffered.

Now the
child opens the
box, which becomes
a mirror. She stares at her
bony self
and does not
look away.

1975

I SIT

Down again.
This baby has
to be
weaned. Don't
bite, baby,
don't pull,
keep still, will
somebody get me
a glass of
water? All
right, baby,
so sweet,
look at that
brown eye
staring at me
over the curve
of my breast.

1970

DAUGHTER

I look
carefully around the
door to see
your face sweet
like a child in a dream
you sleep.
What are
you
dreaming
in your child's mind?
You spent the last hour
of your day
in misery,
toes and knees that hurt,
dolls falling over,
bottles empty;
tears invaded your
cheeks while
over and over
you tossed the blankets off
pleading, *Cover me.*
What's making you cry?
I wanted to know
and held you
as you climbed away
as I sighed,

I'm tired,
let me rest,
go to sleep, my daughter.

1971

SONG

Oh God, she said

It began a beautiful day by the sunup.
And we sat in our grove of trees and smiles
Morning eggs and toast and jam
Long talks and baby babble
Becky sitting in her chair
Spreading goo in her hair.

Oh God, she said, look at the baby

Saying *hi, ho, ha, hi hi, goggydoggymammadada* HI
And the light was coming through the window
Through the handprints on the glass
Making shadow patterns, and the cold day
Was bright outside and they were muddling
In their underwear, getting dressed
Putting diapers on the baby, slipping
Sandals on her feet.

Oh God, she said, look at the baby
He has blood all over him, she cried

Then the postman came
And she went out on the steps
To get her magazine. And they stood
By the stairs and looked, the baby
Tugging at her skirt saying
Mamammama upupup mememe

As she looked at the pictures of Song My.

Oh God, she said, look at the baby
He has blood all over, she cried
Look at that woman's face, my God,
She knows she's going to get it.

Going to get it, they knew
They were going to get it
And it was a beautiful day
The day that began in the fields
With the golden grain against the sky
The babies singing as if there were not
Soldiers in the air.

1969

CHILE

My daughter pleads with me
for the life of our goldfish
souring in a tank
of ancient water,
I want them
to live, she
says.   Late at night
I pass the green tank
still full of guilt.
I have chosen
in the hierarchy of my life
to go to work,
to shop, to cook, to
write these words
before saving the fish;
choices surround me.
Nothing is ever right.
Every breathing space
asks for help;
dust multiplies in the
                    hallway;
lecture notes fly away
through windows which
need glass and paint
and in the back of my mind
somewhere
is a woman
who weeps
for Chile

and shudders at the
executions.
All along she
has been
pondering the social order
and her
worried thoughts
slow
my
every movement.

1975

TORTURE

FOR CAROLYN, CLARIBEL, & MICHELE

Unremembered country

As if taken suddenly
into a strange house
until slowly
you see

you are a part of the tissue
of the lungs
bringing breath
to this body.

What you witness here
is unspeakable

even to speak the words
partakes of the brutality
of the events

that pass between
these couples

the one who inflicts
the one who suffers

with this kind of suffering
the unhealing scar
is visible immediately
you can imagine the white streak
even before the hand moves

that hand
so human
gripping the instrument

does the instrument still
believe in innocence?

All that I know I heard secondhand. Now I am telling you.
Michele came back from Chile with the story of a woman who
was tortured. She spoke to the woman herself. The woman
could not speak of her own torture in any reasonable manner.
Her mind had given way, which is what the torturers wanted.
They knew of this kind of fragility in her. They told her that
her children were dead. This was not true. Michele told us the
woman had an absent look on her face while she told her the
torturers could not be blamed for saying her children were
dead. Michele said she could not forget the expression of this
woman's face; it was beaten down and empty. And in turn, I
cannot forget Michele's voice telling the story, the edge there
of one who has listened and is not certain what can be done,
except to tell, over and over, to tell.

To this I add another story. I heard it from Claribel. She is a
poet. She has told this story herself in her own language, a
very intense Spanish that breaks perhaps even more harshly
over those soft syllables, as she talks about the woman from
Salvador, too ill to torture physically, and how the guards
would rape the other women, and then gathering together the
condoms used in these rapes, thrust them into her mouth.

Only later do I want to ask her how do we tell this story so
that it does not become another facet of the original assault, a
cruelty of words? The question did not arise as she told it, her
face, her hands reaching apologetically for cigarettes, coffee,
those of us who listened, shaking our heads. Phrase by
phrase, carefully each piece of the tale was reconstructed in
this way, as if we were seamstresses assembling garments for
a passage away from or into this life.

The
instruments
the glass cutters
used at Chartres
must have been
sharp
to cut such
clear lines
a range of color
like music.

What, then, shall we do?
Must we have
such lines cut
deeply into
memory
until we know
all the stories
by heart?
Is this

the only way
the suffering
will stop?

I wake very early
a high wind cleans the trees
which sparkle and shine as I
write and then
fall into sleep again, dream.
I have entered
the room of the stories,
outside a woman stands
holding a stopwatch.
As if I have entered
a room full of
radiation, my time
must be limited, but
the clock stops as I
look up. The ceiling
is very high, and
there, at the top
colored windows
let in a choir of light.

1986

GREEN

Trees, grasses, green things!
I am ill.
Memory sticks in me:
my blood
is thick.
Olive tree, this is a sick
being walking here
I cannot remember how
I love you, the breath
I give you is
spotted, oh greenness
a clot
seizes even
my heart, let me
lie down with you
and listen, let me
tell you what I know.

1979

SUMMER NIGHT

This is civilization.
We have inherited it.
We love the glitter.
It is growing dark and trees
crowd the sky.
A pink glow comes to us.
There is a yellow line
we must follow.
Music I find my mouth saying,
Music somewhere back there
in the trees.
Something glowing pulls me
and I whisper *heart*.
But we keep on
don't we, we
keep on down the road.

1983

DEER SKULL

1

I keep placing my hands over
my face, the fingertips just
resting on the place where I feel
my eyebrows and the fine end
of a bone. My eyes are covered
with the blood of my hands, my
palms hold
my jaws. I do this at dinner.
My daughter asks
Are you all right?
and by a common miracle
when I smile
she knows I am.

2

I ask her what she will do
after we eat. Sleep she
tells me. But I will clean
the deer skull, wash it.

3

You gave me this skull in the woods
told me to bring it clean
and tell the story I had told you
before, about how the deer had
come to me, and I said I would.

4

And I put this skull on an old
newspaper, pulled the lower part
of the jaws free, touched it first
carefully, as if it would fall apart
in my hands, the bone paper-
thin, and then I saw I could
scrub, so brushed the surface with
steel and my fingers and more
and more this surface became
familiar to me.

5

I wanted to see the lines of it
what it would be if it had been
polished by the wind, the water,
and my hands, these agents making
the skull more itself.
Slowly I was not afraid at all
and my fingers went into the deepest
holes of this thing, not afraid
for myself or it, feeling
suddenly as if cleaning this
small fragment of earth away
from the crevices inside was
like loving.

6

But it was when I touched the place
where the eyes were that I knew
this was the shell of the deer that had
lived here, this was this deer
and not this deer, her home and
now empty of her, but not
empty of her, I knew also, not
empty of her, as my hands
trembled.

7

And in that instant remembered you
had been in that body of
that deer dying, what
does it feel like to be a deer
dying, the death consumes
you like birth, you are
nowhere else but in the center.

8

Remembering those gentle deer
that watched me as I wept,
or the deer that leapt as if
out of my mind, when I saw
speaking there in that green place
the authority of the heart
and the deer of the woods where
my feet stood, stared at me until

I whispered to her and cried
at her presence.

9

And when I cleaned the skull
I washed myself and sat
my body half out of the water
and put my hands again over
my face, my fingers edging the
bone over my eyes, and I thought
how good this feels and this
is a gesture you make.

10

Tell this story of the deer's skull
you asked quietly and so I
came in my own time to put
these words carefully here
slowly listing each motion
on this thin paper
as fragile and as tough
as knowledge.

1978

KNOWLEDGE OF THE BODY

1

This is knowledge of the body,
how holding is like being held
how being held is like holding.
Miracles enter my body,
miracles enter your body.
How the sight of two bodies holding
comes into the body seeing
so that what is held back
would be given to the air
as tears or softness.

2

Each place with a message,
spaces between the ribs, crevice
inside the elbow, ridge above the
eye, two points on each side of
the ankle, skin between the thumb
and finger, the seventh vertebra,
soft hairs along the spine.

3

Even the knowledge the body has
when it dies or what the eyes
see in another's death;
what is gone then forever
coming back in dreams that tell
the story of leaving, the body holding,
in wells of movement and stillness,

grieving and
the testimony of what the body
could not do:
how the body has knowledge of
what cannot be done
so that the magnitude of all that is not
in the body, lives in the body.

4

Touch
your hand
to my face that way
and you are
touching me
she whispered.

5

The body wishing for more than the eyes
see the way the lungs insist
on truth and will not
breathe for less.

6

Touch
way to the well of me
she said
skin rising
when there was only
the thought of a hand

and then only a hand and
the surprising vision of flesh.

7

Breast against arm, head in the hollow
of thigh, the underside of her
arm not moving, but still moving.
The most still, the dead. Miracles
enter and leave
our bodies. Miracles enter and leave
Your body, and the body is
never still until in that moment
between breaths we see not
with our eyes.

8

And if you are there
behind your skin
and if there are tears behind your tears
and if there is speaking behind
your speaking

9

Let me hold all these her body
entered her voice and asked
as if holding this truth
of another woman
was like being held, and feeling
the softness of herself enter the air

she put her hand on the bone
of her own cheek and was
held by the knowledge of her body:
how being held is like holding.

1979

THREE SHADES OF LIGHT
ON THE WINDOWSILL

I was already
years old when these things
began to happen to me which
must happen to every child.
As when her voice singing
turned my body
into a tremor in the
place where I stood
as when
reaching for myself
in the darkness
I became blood, as when
I woke saying
oh, delighted
by three shades of light
on the windowsill.

1978

THREE LOVE POEMS

✻ ✻ ✻

The sweet soul is sexual, we say
lost in each other, what he called
id is so much more and
no object in the universe travels faster
than the speed of light, we whisper,
love, this motion of light
does not change, I see it
in the saying of it to you,
I hear in your hearing
your hands find me saying
yes, how everything,
I could die, fits together,
and the sweet soul
is so large, so large, and hold
me so that bone bursts upon bone
and this is the bone of your face
I say astonished, let me be
possessed by astonishment
of you, your being and the history
of your bright speech breaking in me
as light on every distant feeling,
the story of how you came here
evokes to fullness in me, taste
and take into your mouth, love, this sweetness
your sweetness you have made in me,
we say, shuddering, delight.

↓↓↓

You suddenly like
Einstein in this picture the
power of his vision making his
body almost frail like
light shining through his ribs
only he smiles and his hand
touches his lips and he thinks
with enormous pleasure of all the
clutter of papers surrounding
his lucid joy and you
smiled turning your head quickly
back in the midst of one flash
of knowledge between us to
tell your daughter the time of
her birth and then that birth
played over the bones of your
shoulders so quickly its power
making you instantly small
you looked then smiling at me
hands on the wheel and changing
gears, laughing because you had
forgotten the money your mind
at the same time studying this
fact and all its intricate
being radiant between us your
daughter's intelligence measuring

stars and we vibrant with
meaning with where this car
is taking us.

Love for you sucks me like a
light-winged being or the petals of
a bloom floating back on a warm wind
into this house of my own language
where you would know me, where you might
find me should some thread of me uncoil
in you, should you want me,
but where I refuse to wait and refusing
drive through the force of my longing
for you, into myself, finding
a secret solitude and my own meanings
and I shudder with unfaithful joy even
in being here alone: how the world
swims in my eyes, now a clear and objective
presence, gleaming, as if I had not
seen the faces of things before,
nor light, and such
extraordinary music strains the walls –
I see even the cat dances, and almost
say, I have not *seen* this cat dance
before, when suddenly in the
kitchen, *Kim*, a voice rushes the sound
of your name into the air, and this
air, this solitary air fills
with tears to know you, thus.

1979

A STORY

My mind is etching a place
full of dark lines
where you and I slept together
like sheep and the body
of a mother lay between
and the past like a coal
sat inside you
(as if you had eaten ash).

And this couple is etched in the center
of a story: I peer
in the shadows and as if through
a window am carried
back to the heart of a night
I slept near you thinking
I had captured nearness
forever.

See how ignorant the
bodies of sleepers
and how you
ignorant are sleeping
still when I
have walked to the window,
how the story tells
of weeping and ruin
how the blackness of lines
keeps saying

The story is ended,
I call to you
ended but you
unhearing and curled in
sameness, you mute sheep darken
the form.

1976

DREAM

Moving through the rooms of this
real house, I walk
through corridors of dream
where old wounds open
like windows, like doors.
Here a light glares,
here a voice calls,
here a child hides
beneath the enormous wave.

What is it like to leave?
What is it like to be left behind?

Like a house on fire, like a
cinder burning a place
of terror, making
a place
of prayer.

What did I do?
Nothing.
Nothing more than you had to do
being who you are.
Who am I?
No one more than you had
to be.
No one.

1983

MOVE

The little kitchen objects are distraught.
I'm not at home,
cries the peeler.
The paring knife is anxious
to be out so late
and shudders,
This is against the rules.
Soup ladle, saltshaker,
all of them sing,
We are naughty!
We are lost!
What will become of us
in these strange rooms?

1983

DOOR

I bring you memories
like gifts
a blind kicking at doors,
the back of a house.
The word *dumpling*
pulls at me, and I say to you
against a deep and silent vow
I took back then
I did forget
I was ever a child.

1978

UNDER

There are terrors that terrorists fear.
Under the exploded building,
nothing, rooms,
a hand, *a* child's bed.
And over that another
where a sister slept,
and a box of toys,
and a window full of night.
One must forget such rooms
ever existed.
For the mother left,
and the father and the sister
and the room
never existed again.
Then time stopped
and terror began.

1983

✹✹✹

My daughter is hungry
for more
and should it surprise you
this pleases her mother?
I soak the bread in
egg whispering under
my breath
growing bones.
Over my desk
infant eyes stare.

1983

My child deep
in the snow of illusion
thinks she's guilty
(for more than can be said).
The argument, the loss.
A hatred here or there.
All terrible. All terrible
the things we know,
these things we never show
and children suffer.

1984

THE PERFECT MOTHER

1

The perfect mother lets the cat
sleep on her head. The
children laugh.
Where is she?
She is not in the sandbox.
She is not carefully ironing the starched
ruffles of a Sunday dress.
What does she say?
She does not speak.
Her head is under the cat and
like the cat, she sleeps.

2

But her children are in a marsh!
Bogged, they have gone wild.
Yet, no one should worry.
See, they are there, in a sunny kitchen.
They drink cups of soup and wipe
their faces with yellow napkins.
What does it matter if
they are hatching plots, if
in their waking dreams
the poor cat is trapped
its hair
standing on end?

3

Where shall we go? We ask the perfect
mother. What
do you want of us? She is no
where to be found.
Not in the cookie jar
we have broken to bits
not under the shiny kitchen floor
not on our lips.
Here we are transfixed,
mourning the perfect mother, and she
is caught in the trapped cat
of her children's dreams.

1984

THE BAD MOTHER

The bad mother wakes from dreams
of imperfection trying to be perfection.
All night she's engineered a train
too heavy with supplies
to the interior. She fails.
The child she loves
has taken on bad habits, cigarettes
maybe even drugs. She
recognizes lies. *You don't
fool me,* she wants to say,
the bad mother, ready to play
and win.
This lamb who's gone –
this infant she is
pinioned to – does not listen,
she drives with all her magic down a
different route to darkness where
all life begins.

1984

TWO, HERS AND MINE

I had a child who delighted me
everyday her growth
and grown she has become
wondrously forgiving
to all my errors that worked
in her life like thorns
giving us both a time
of rusty pain, for me
thrown back again to
infancy and all
that was done to me, the
harshest music of that truth
played out in lives
two, hers and mine
leaping as you could not have thought
quicker than the eye.

1984

OUR MOTHER

Pot of Tea

Our mother makes a pot of tea.
Watch this, she says,
It is a love affair.
When the leaves and the water meet
they see something in each other,
they become alike.
She holds the teacup close
to our noses.
A wet heat rises up in the
air and touches us.

Oil

In other places
the trees are pruned
and branches are hit
to make the olives fall.
Not here. Here
we leave the trees alone
and pick up what falls.
We say, *Trees can take revenge*.
You cannot help but stop and stare
at the shapes the trees make.
And what's that smell?
Oil?
Our mother cuts up tomatoes
and cucumbers.
She pulls a weed
at the side of the road.
Oregano Oregano
she repeats
trying as usual
to teach us.

Tissue

Our mother tells us it is time to clean up.
She gives us a box of tissue.
She shows us how to blow our noses.
If we weep a little
she makes us tell why
and dries our eyes.
If we go to the bathroom
she gives us tissue.
We have turned over
our glass of milk on the table.
Wipe, she says.
Standing in a dark closet
she arranges the boxes in a tall pile.
The old tissue goes outside.
Into the fire, she says.

Teeth

She who usually feeds us
is in a bad mood.
Are you trying to eat me up?
she shouts.
She bares her teeth
and makes a low noise.
With a disgusted gesture
she tells us
Go study your manners.
And wipe your feet,
she adds.

Dogs

Don't be afraid, she tells us.
Don't let them best you.
We are trembling.
We have burst into tears.
Here, she says, *I've been afraid
once too,* she says,
and there is another way up the hill.
She gives us water.
*Maybe you're not ready
yet,* she says to herself,
to face them.

Distress

What would our mother say?
Where is our mother?
Does she know?
Does she know what is happening to us
here?
What will she do?
Will she save us? Will she come for us?
Does she know what happens to us
here?
Is it happening to her?
To her, to her, too?

Our Mother Talks about Metaphor

Our mother cautions us.
Think of this, she says,
every time you turn around
certain you have lost something
afraid you have left it behind,
you have
you have.
But, she says solemnly, *you must*
not ask where it is,
pronouncing her words distinctly
so we get her meaning,
You must ask what *it is.*
She smiles.
What have you lost?
What?

Stories and Poems

One after another
our mother helps us to write
our little poems.
She says she likes them.
She says this is good you should
write down what I say.
She says *If it weren't for stories and poems*
if it weren't for stories and poems
but she never finishes this sentence.
She only raises her eyebrows.
And you, she says, *you never finish*
your sentence either, crying,
Mother, mother
give us
give us

Sleep

We are going to sleep now.
Our mother takes us in her open arms.
She promises us soft breasts.
She will stroke our heads.
She will hide us in blankets.
She will fill our mouths.
Our mother will do all this for us.
Whether we have been bad or good
She will take us.

Our Mother

At the center of the earth there is a mother.
If any of us who are her children choose to die
she feels a grief like a wound deeper
than any of us can imagine.
She puts her hands to her face
like this: her palms open.
Put them there as she does.
Her fingers press into her eyes.
Do that, too.
She tries to howl.
Some of us have decided
this mother cannot hear all of us
in our desperate wishes.
Here, in this time,
our hearts have been cut into small chambers
like ration cards
and we can no longer imagine every
morsel nor each tiny
thought at once,
as *she* still can.
This is normal,
she tries to tell us,
but we don't listen.
Sometimes someone has a faint memory
of all this, and
she suffers.
She is wrong to imagine

she suffers alone.
Do you think we are not all hearing and speaking
at the same time?
Our mother is somber.
She is thinking.
She puts her big ear
against the sky
to comfort herself.
Do this. She calls to us,
Do this.

1982

PRAYER FOR CONTINUATION

There is a record
I wish to make here.
A life.
And not this life alone
but the thread
which keeps shining
like gold floss woven into cloth
which catches your eyes
and you are won over.

Kyrie eleison
Baruch atah
Hosanna   Adonai
Om mani
Gloria
Padme hum
Nam Myoho
Renge Kyo
Galan
galancillo.
Do you love
this world?

Where is the point I can enter?
Where is the place I can touch?

Let me tell you
I am so serious

and taking aim
like a woman with a bow
eyes looking silently
at each space between the trees
for movement.

2

I cannot begin now.
I do not wish to write these numbers
on this page here.
224 warheads destroy
every Soviet city with a population
over 100,000.
But once I begin writing
the figures do not stop.
A twenty megaton
bomb, a firestorm rages over
3,000 acres.
A 1,000 megaton bomb
destroys
California,
Nevada, Utah, Oregon,
Puget Sound.
Destroys.
California.

3

Thirty-seven days from my
fortieth birthday. I have
gone up and down this coast

so many times I could trace
the shape of it for you
with my hands, up
into the high cold trees, down
to warm water and
the sprawling city
where I was
born, 1943.
In that year
while I slept
not entirely wanted
in a still room
behind venetian blinds
somewhere in a foreign language
babies were set on fire.
Their cries did not wake me.
Only I breathed in the dust
of their deaths.

4

It is my love I hold back
hide
not wanting to be seen
scrawl of hand
writing
don't guess
don't guess at my
passion
a wholly wild and raging
love for this world.

(Home)
If you look in this block
in the North of California
you will find a house
perhaps a century old
with the original wood shingles
dark from years of sun
and fine old joints: the men
who made them are dead, the attic
made into a bedroom now, the
linoleum added in 1955.
Twenty years ago
I lived there, a student
studying the history of
Western Civilization, reading John Milton,
looking out the attic window
at a cement sidewalk
that was before just a
dirt path
and Spanish, and was before
perhaps a forest or a
meadow, a field,
belonging to the Ohlone
who have all,
even their children,
even all traces of who they were,
perished
from our memory.

6

This is the world I was born into.
Very young I learned
my mother and my father
had a terrible sorrow.
And very young
I learned this sorrow from them.

7

The mind is vast
what we know small.
Do you think we are not all
sewn together?
I still argue with her
grit my teeth trying to feel
the pain that riddled her body
the day they told her
she would never walk.
I try to enter her mind
the night she took her own life.

Cells have memory!
I shout to her.
Science gave you
an unnecessary despair.

8

Nor do they argue
nor do they understand

nor do they know
but still it is so.
And there are structures of
unknowing
we call disbelief.

9

Every American city
with a population above
25,000
targeted.
A bomb with the
explosive power
of 20 million tons of TNT.
80 percent of all cancers.
How is it,
this woman asks,
the brilliant efforts of
American scientists
have been put
to such destructive uses?

10

It is not real, they tell us,
this home we long for
but a dream of a place
that never
existed.
But it is so familiar!

And the longing in us is
ourselves.

11

This is the world I was born into.
I saw the wave and its white curl.
I saw branches coming from trees
like streams from rivers.
And the water poisoned
and the land.
I saw the whale leap out of the water
I saw my child's eyes come out of me
                    her first cry.
And the air, the rain acid.

Kyrie eleison
Baruch atah
Hosanna
Adonai
Do you love the world?

12

Suppose she lay down her bow.
And went into
that place
stepping so slowly
so surely.

13

This is what I wanted to tell you.
This is what I wanted to say.
Words come late and dark
near sleep.
She said to me
my head was eating my heart.
And what is good?
What is bad?
The delicacy of transmission.
Old alliances fracture
like the cold branches of a
winter tree.
This is the closest I can get.
The world is washed in space.
It is the words she used
precisely those
and I could not remember them.
Only my conviction.
There was badness and goodness.
One was bad.
The other suffered.
And I wanted to
I wanted to mend her.
She told me the whole story
and I told her what was
good and what was bad,
and this was not what she needed.

You think I am trying
to throw away morality
but I am not.
I am not trying to
throw away caring.
In a dream
I see myself
a handsome man
walking without feeling
into a desert.
I am not like him
yet this dream comes to me
and I feel grief.
Out at the edge of this territory
is a missile.
I know for certain
this weapon is bad.
I do not try to mend her
and this makes me weep
for what she has suffered.

14

(The Enemy)
I wanted you to be good.
I wanted your judgments.
But all your rules became ash.
Your goodness was like an island.
(Your sainthood *was* the sin.)
Now that you have fallen

I cross the water
wrestle with you
charge you to bless me
watch as you
appear and disappear
become me.

15

The mind is vast.
A whale blows.
Shall we pitch ourselves into terror?
Shall we come home?
Enter darkness, weep,
know the dimension
of absence, the unreachable deep.

16

How far can they go?
This is my speech
an American speech of whalers
and farmers, what my
people did,
plain, simple, honed
to the point
how far will they go?
Is there a stopping point?
Everyone knows there is not.

17

What can we make of this?
Two children held hostage together
in a van
for ten months.
What kind of man?
A girl, born three years ago
in California,
a boy who was born in
and survived Vietnam.
How far?
The children were continually beaten
with a rubber hose
and forced into sexual acts
in exchange for being fed.
I am a woman
who reads this story
in a newspaper.

18

(Bone Cancer)
You must not let terror overtake you.
It is a bone breaking in the middle of the night.
It is a misspelled word.
It is everything you thought you knew
becoming unknown, the leaves
stripped from the tree,
all the greenness orange and dry,
it is pain past bearable, you must not.

Down the street in the darkness someone young
is dying. The soil, perhaps, under your feet
is poison, the water you drink.
What is this? Be reasonable. Disaster
is always predicted and look
we exist. Humanity had a day of birth,
slow, unreasoned, surprising. Now,
is it possible, is it possible
could this be?

19

Do we not want
this place
to find it
the body again
hearth, heart.
How is it I can say this
so that you will
see too what I have seen.
After the fires
(after the unspeakable)
there will be no home.
And what of us
will remain in memory?
Nothing?

20

At least we think of them.
The six million.

We long for them.
Want them to be like they were
before
want the music
their mothers and fathers sang
to pass from our lips.
And we ask
How is it they did not know?

21

Do you think it is right
to despair?
No, no, it is not about
right and wrong.
It is the thread
shining.

22

Kyrie eleison
Baruch atah Adonai
Om mani
New rules
Padme hum
take the place of the old.
Be Here Now
is the lesson.
But I do not want to be.
I am one hundred years away
into the future.

My heart aches wondering.
Will this old tree grow even bigger?
Will its roots threaten the foundation of
                this house?
Will there be a daughter of a
        daughter of a daughter
        a son? And what is the
look in their eyes? Tell me
what you see there. And
do you like to watch
them as they walk across
fields.

Fields?

1982

BEECH

A woman is walking up a hill.
Trees, their glory, move in her eyes.
She moves slowly, she has been ill
and asks, *Is this what makes you wise?*
How can you estimate or measure
pain, all night a kind of border
to the unremembered place of pleasure
and the distant want inside her.
The first sign of life is thought,
she thinks, though this may not be right,
not the language, though she does not doubt
the act itself, its nature, like light
wanting to find, wanting to make lucid
this that is loved, a caress
for what is here, nothing invalid,
just the atmosphere, to bless
and be blessed by speech.
My God, what is it, every step.
What would you call this white wood, *beech?*
Or the night that luminescence now accepts,
she whose heart has felt its way along the edges
over the whole plain of being, the breadth.

1986

ATMOSPHERE

Learning to
draw tenderness, the
sky is full of
snow for her,
and she knows the
road curves around
her and the chill
of the air has no
fear, and she
sees her sorrow
gleaming in the
hardening river, she is
learning to take
tenderness from the
atmosphere.

1978

FIELDS

Fields, grasses
growing things
I will never be the same
I have become one of you
I have become like you.

1978

I WAKE THINKING OF
MYSELF AS A MAN

And as I rise slapping my feet
on the wooden floor
I begin to imagine myself
quite tall
with broad shoulders, a
painter who puts his feet
into dirty tennis shoes, does
not comb his hair and lumbers
largely into the kitchen, laces
loose in all this space.
I am this man, giant in my
female house, as I eat
my huge hands dwarf these bowls,
this breakfast!
I have become so big
I need a larger meal, more
eggs, coffee, and the newspaper
the newspaper rests like a
delicate letter in
my enormous grasp.

1986

BORN INTO A
WORLD KNOWING

This will happen
Oh god we say just give
me a few more
breaths
and don't let it be
terrible
let it be soft
perhaps in someone's
arms, perhaps tasting
chocolate
perhaps
laughing or asking
Is it over already?
or saying *not yet. Not*
yet the sky
has at this moment turned
another shade of blue,
and see there a child
still plays
in the fresh snow.

1985

WHAT YOU WORE THAT DAY

Something in the way she
would place a cup
on the table, pause,
smile,
saunter back to the
stove, hands flying
while we waited for the water.
Yesterday I finally
had to wash
the dishes, soak that
shirt I wore.
Something in the way
she came to this kitchen saying
no eggs, just
bread, laughing.
I brought her towel
up here, as if
she'd given it to me,
dried my face.
Something in the way
what she wore that day
before she left flung
out on the bed, shoes
kicked at the edge of
the blanket breathing
like two lungs exhaled,
waiting.

1985

117

ABSENCE

You still think of those who
have died, and I tell you, *Don't worry,*
we have their absence,
and music is as sensual as ever
sliding like a tongue
over the ear that first heard
the words of death.
What would you call this?
You could perhaps say anything.
That it is winter now
but still warm, that there are
two kinds of butter, one called
sweet, that the heart
you have come to think of
as your own
keeps beating.

1985

NATURE

... nature is neither good nor bad,
but it is; it exists and endures.

GEORGE SAND TO GUSTAVE FLAUBERT

1

The morning is cold.
This is the forty-third year
of my life.
I write to you as to
an infinitely loving friend
kept apart from me
by circumstance
but still listening
and, in a way, speaking
with a voice softened by
perspective, you
who are not in the thick
of events.

Where is it I can start?
The tears belong to my childhood.
I have known this for a long time.
A few nights ago
I saw myself as
a plaza
very late at night
moonlight shining from a side alley
a door perhaps closing along an avenue behind
a footstep, fast, going away
a wind which moves
one piece of paper around
the bone-white base of the fountain

that at this hour
has no water and is quiet.

I was raised to believe
the world will always stay
well-oiled, smooth
as an advertisement,
perfect and the worry
perpetually accompanying
my grandmother's life was just
the engine of this perfection.
Death, yes,
there was death, and loss
terrible loss, we
watched open eyed and shaking
as they happened to us.
But these events were errors, and
did not belong in my life.

2

Shall I write that I am lonely?
You must know this.
I who love to eat breakfast
and spread out the newspapers
talking until noon.

Shall I tell you how many
months I have been ill?
And that I have learned many

new routes into our
endless curiosity about
existence. How the sharpest pain
takes you like a lover, leaves
no room for any other desire
except absence. How what is more subtle
erodes   leaves you
suspended somewhere
outside what you have always
called real.
Shall I tell you this illness
came after a shock, a
death?

To report these events
is to report nothing.
My life has been a tide
moving in response
to what happens, and yet
speaking as I do now
I feel I have never attempted
to speak at all before.

At the center of
all my sorrows
I have felt a presence
that was not mine alone.

When I spoke to you
about grief
I forgot to say
how large grief is
how to suffer it
is to descend into a canyon.
You will look upward for miles
at ancient walls
as if at an unfathomable history
that is your history too
and just beginning to
take shape in your mind.

In a film I saw a
man say his evening prayers
in another language
and I thought
this is what I should do,
as if I had a prayer to say
in a strange language
whose words I could not explain
but only feel.

3

Do you know what I mean
when I say
I have discovered that
this is simply true:
if there is a hand that feeds us

sometimes this hand will give us
emptiness.

When I was younger
I walked into a plaza.
Then it was not a dream
and I was not alone.
There was a hand in my hand.
A fountain cascaded through
the city light. Near the edge
a man was sitting.
He sang songs in a foreign tongue.
The square was filled with others who,
like me, stopped to listen.
Much later I learned
that his song which seemed to climb
higher and higher even toward flight
was a song of loss.

I do not know how to end this speech.
You who are so far away
will you hear me?
I am thinking of call and response.
Can it be that you will answer me?
The space between us is so vast
perhaps by the time
your voice is here
all the configurations of my life
will have changed.

All I will be able to do then
is to tell a new story.
Speak then, friend, you
who have all along been listening
and seeing
how it is that
we continue.

1986

꙳꙳꙳

Quiet, quiet heart
she is not ready
let her sleep a while longer.
You can imagine
her sleeping face.
Just think
you who are already awake
this alone
nearly sweeps you away.

1986

✸✸✸

I wake to your gestures
which break over me
like honey.
You who are uncertain
pull me as certainly
into you
as gravity.
Am I this gravity
in my dream of you
or the one who
supple as a branch makes
her way unerring
to earth.

1986

CONFESSION

I wasn't any saint
I burned with earth
and cried
and bit what I could bite
and shied, strange
animal at phantoms of myself
dreaming what
could not be
and felt a sting
between my thighs
for days I would not
touch, taking
vengeance
for my loneliness.

1987

AMNESIA

You have deserted yourself, gone
deep into the mind of an
amnesiac, that one you thought
you had something with,
what should you ask of your own
nonexistence, testimony? A
portrait? The picture
for example of the goat's head
perpetually eating a wildflower
who stares with an ignorant look
from the surface of your desk.
Things are not always
the way they are supposed to be.
You are trying to search
for endings, to call things
this or that, when you ought
to walk across the room,
open a book, go out even
to the corner, stand for a moment.
We are only impressions
that change
not just daily but
at every moment.
You tell this to someone who calls.
He is feeling what you are feeling.
What we think of as interruption,
you say, is substance.
Try to remember, you speak now to yourself,
who were you before you took flight?

You were the one who would one day
take flight. Laugh, you say,
look at the goat's head, you are
fond of it, you like to think of it
eating paper, eating everything, all
you have ever imagined, yourself,
the one who does not remember,
and there in the goat's stomach
or in the grass, the soil where the
goat stands, you and she will
find yourselves, the ones you abandoned,
the world.

1987

HAPPINESS

for Barbara Green

Happiness. I am not used
to this. (There is always
something wrong.)
Look at it
the bright early tree.
(I am trying to find out
how you fell.)
The leaves have already turned.
(I want you to see
this, how they
glow outside the glass.)
Morning light strikes
differently. For so
many years I hardly
had time to know such
moments. They struck me
with such intensity
I would have said
battered me open.
I never understood
they were mine.
I was panicked.
Unhappiness caught up with me
all the time.
Did you know
the speed of light never alters
even when you go faster
it will be
still that much faster

than you?
(I am thinking that in your fall
something momentous occurred.)
What I see as beautiful
I want you to see too.
Next door, the workmen are hammering.
Very soon we'll all go to lunch.
For some reason this moves me to tears.
How life is.
(One does not have to explain
what occurs. One only need say
it has meaning.)
Years ago, when I was young
I traveled to Italy, took in
the great sights. I was in awe, yet
I did not understand
seeing Masaccio's frescoes
fading like shadows into the walls,
this would be the only time
nor that
I would never forget.
Those muted shades are
still with me, as possession
and longing, and the view too
of the square before that church
the air, newly spring,
that day, all of it.
Life, I have finally begun to realize,
is real.

(All this time you recover
from falling
will sink indelibly into mind.)
The leaves
may fall before you are able
to see them. Science
has recently learned
the line
of existence is soft
and stretches out like a field
wind and light shaping the grass
energy
of sight giving consciousness
force. In the meantime
we live out our lives.
(This morning we talked for so long
everything became lucid.
How can I say what I see?)
At each turning
perfection eludes me.
One moment is not like another.
Last spring
the house next door caught fire.
There was the smell of gas.
We thought
both houses would go.
I vanished up the hill,
went to the house of a friend
where we listened for flames

and to that aria from Italian
opera, was it the one of love,
or jealousy, or grief?
My house was untouched.
Now the one next door is painted,
fixed. In place of
perfection, the empty hands
I turned out to the world
are filled.
With what? A letter
half written, the notes
I make on this page,
this new feeling about my shoulders
of age, that sad child's story
you told me this morning,
the workmen's tools sounding
and stopping. What? As time
moves through me, does it also
move through you?
I keep remembering what you said,
ways you have of seeing (and that
light must have curved with
your fall). This
is the paradox of vision:
Sharp perception softens
our existence in the world.

1986

LAKE

I sleep and wake into desire of you.
You are always at the edge of dream.
Your presence makes a hidden lake
even my mother's drinking cannot stain.
The way we turn to each other,
all our woes, bodies of water stream
to the surface and breathe.
What your father did to you
cannot sustain.
The darkened hold unheld
washes between us wet
in flesh and close,
until drenched
in the heat of speech
we are deluged,
forced, pitched,
quickened
past the last compromise,
pressed into cries.
Dimensions break and reassemble
and everything
is soft with want.

1990

HOMOEROTIC POEM

Wildness in me opens
wide a mouth with
the texture of marsh.
The pond on the surface
calm, I could
go out with my tongue
fierce and flickering.
Nothing needs to be made.
I am already here
body submerged then liquid.
Continuous heart beat now
and teeth.
Oh the pressure
of bone emerging white
in the angle of hip.
What I cannot see
through the murky deep,
fish suspended
among the reeds and algae
slide and squirm
into me.
Putting the tip of myself
into the maw
I am silvery, steamed
gorged, tongued.

1990

THE SWAY

I have been waiting all day
for you to place
your tongue in your mouth
in a particular way.
What do I care
if my body decays?
The blue vein in my wrist
is new today.
Oh pray let it be free and unique
the thought of your lips
as they stay
just here against the lingering
pulse of my mouth
while you are away
in the imponderable
field that will
catch us both,
the sway.

1991

SMALL

Trying to peel
apart and grasp
the fluttering ends
of memory, you
tell me
you were so small
and the hand so large
your face was
nearly covered,
when he came
to pull you
into his power.

1993

A GANGSTER MOVIE

In the beginning there is just
darkness.
Then the shadows yield
to light.
Names will follow.
Who did what
and if not why,
well, then we hope
we'll care.
Next is the action.
Not very nice
        (things taken, greed
        lots of
        blood
        bodies falling)
but large and
pleasurable to
imagine.
Perhaps it's the
clean line of vision:
we see all of it happen.
And as for what lies beyond
the scope of witness
this is portended beautifully;
we are given artful hints
the feeling, strangely,
that we already know
what rests unspoken

in the growing shadows
before the dark
returns again.

1989

GOD

I am a bevy of young pigs
and the green snake
devours us.

I am a pair of ducks
exquisitely feathered
breasts torn out
by two ancient
snapping turtles.

I am a child looking
for good
as leopards
leap from every direction.

I would like to put
my face between
the breasts
of God.

Has she gone
only so we
can call for
Her return?

I am a woman
in the midst of life
with things uncovered
things undone.

1989–1997

GONE

Anger and the dead TV
mixed up love and
pity me
part of a history
I can't forget
rolled into to one
with old cigarettes
late-night bourbon
and the reclining chair,
a half century
gone. So long
since I
sat opposite
and afraid of you
my child's mind trapped
in your loosened eyes
as you aimed your
wild conjectures
at me.

Who was she
the one you were?
You changed.
Time passed.
Memory faded in me.

Though I played the scene
with others again
placing myself

at the wrong end,
a refracted sight,
unwilling mirror of
a lover's
reflection, who she
thought I was.

You and I
left those roles
but even released
from the sour frame
the bitter scent remains.

Somewhere the glowing
screen, the liquor bottle,
the stale ash still
exist, all wrapped
in the same old skein of pity.

Yet the story is good
the rhythm of telling strong,
the almost casual
arrangement of things
makes
the period come alive,
and as with
the setting for a film
gives me a certain fondness
even for bad times.

You are gone now,
except in memory and
loving you, I am
the one remembering.
But over time, a century,
when I am memory too
those painful nights,
even the plotline
will vanish like
they never were. The
scene will be outmoded, then a
curiosity. Just love
and vision will be left
to burn into the center
where, at last,
the stage is empty.

1997

STIRRING

The sugar and infliction
of your love,
what a mix
the history
of your being, all your
young years here.
The flash
did quicken but
was followed by a
freeze.
Something cold
in me met
your dizzying
swing with
the lumbering sway
of hibernation.

My own young years were
also strung between
a mother's turns
knit one
purl two
first kind
then cruel.

The stitch that
bound us
lost now,
cold wakes me

to see
what passed
between
good, bad
nothing indifferent
everything finished
but the finish rough.

Still texture has its
reason, is the
stuff of story
and in a season
tastes of infinity
sweet, fresh
memory.

1996

NIGHT

Like a stick bent
and chewing its own bark,
crazy and bright with
wakefulness,
seeing what I would not see
before,
all activity,
response, alarm,
words said months ago
the spite,
those narrow slicing
glances
slicing still
the rhythm of my
breath.
Skillful you
dodged the echo
without a mark
that shows, even
aiming at the next,
while I still mouthed
shock.
The form was love.
Red with want
and wanting more
blue with the mysterious

bruise of loss
primary as light, as every morning and
the sure descent of night.

1996

THE GROUP

The subject isn't nice
the theme not pretty.
How can you shape or scan
the way they ganged
up on you
and just at your
weakest moment.
With their lumbering
lopsided logic
they made you feel
small like a flea
without agility.
Flat and sad,
you were no match for them.
But when you abandoned
hope and let time pass
you could see
the lurching and lunging
at shadows they do
toward any passing fancy
(not just you)
as part of a larger plan.
A plan of course that
is never fully done.
There will always be
another one.

1997

THE SPELL

It is a cold day
which you can love
if you steady your eyes

In its own way
mild
soft body of gauze

Pale chiffon. You
remember
waking to this sky

In another place,
how the stone held
the gray and the grace

The bridge over the
water, the shine a
sweet embrace.

Someone must break
the spell
telling what she

Knows, somber
to witness, panic
to hide or protect

Even muted or
wanting to save the
union

Words would
be quick and
almost violent.

3

Not the facts
but the
texture

Not what
was said but
the look that

Played in the eyes
is what was given
you to read.

Having failed at
the proof you knew
you wanted

Finally you see
truth was the lover
who never strayed.

1997

CURVE

FOR ALICE STEWART

Using the language of science
she showed us the steep curve
mysterious on the graph
pointing to casualties of a certain kind.
Only over time
did the idea come to her, hidden
under this curve early deaths
of another sort produced a different but
invisible curve
making it
one long slope of dying.
All this proceeded
in a now to be calculated way
after the first explosion
began the chain of events
diminishment, loss
collapse, cancer
the disappearance of
family, friends.
Genetics? she said.
The children
the ones born later?
Yes, but that
is another study.
Perhaps next time,
another lecture.
The consequences
grim as they are
sterling clear.

There to see in the numbers,
one might easily infer
the stories,
the telling
blank spaces.

1988

SHE TRIES TO REASON IT OUT

No thinking occurs this way of course. Along a perfectly clear, straight line leading from one point to another, to the next and then the next, until there is a neat conclusion. The idea of an irrefutable finding discovered by unbroken increments of logic is an illusion. Even the most analytical thought is more serpentine than this. Time interposes. Sleep. Dreams. You muse. You stare. In the course of two hours you follow several leads, meet several dead ends and then, defeated and hungry, you stop to take a meal. Which will be something you threw together cleverly using the last bit of lettuce, since you have not driven down the hill to the market in several days, and there isn't any lettuce in the garden; there is hardly any garden at all, because you need to improve the soil and you can't do that now, it's been raining, which is just as well since you haven't the money to spend; and though you miss that connection between the ground you are standing on and the food you eat you're glad for these last three leaves, and the bit of leftover chicken you can add.

But the meal, the filled feeling, the good taste of it, makes you a bit sleepy. You lie down maybe on the bed or maybe on the couch. You look at catalogs. You like to do this because the content of them is sufficiently far away from what you're trying to think through, and you are distracted. Which seems appropriate. To go any further now you have somehow got to untie the knot of yourself. There is the gardener's catalog with its beautiful clay-sculpted borders you know you will never buy yet you like looking at the picture of them. Thinking. Imagining how they would be in your garden. Too stiff you think. A bit too formal. Then you shut your eyes. The pillow seems to swim but you know it's really you, your consciousness, moving off into that other space, the sleepy space and then suddenly you are awake again.

And what is it? You can hardly remember what the problem was. What you were thinking about. So you shake the last remnants of sleep off and climb the stairs and there it is, a bit bracing, the last sentence. And you can see that this was the problem. This last sentence turns you in the wrong direction. It sailed out of the sentence before without skipping even a beat but that was the problem. It was rote. As sleek and shiny as you were able to make it, the words too facile, it had lost contact with the ground of your thought. And you knew it not because you could see the illogic of it, which you couldn't then, not yet, but because it had a certain dullness under the shine. That spark of recognition which only comes when the words somehow hold a trace of all that you know that cannot quite be put into words was missing.

And from this false start, this mistaken direction there would have been no way to make that parabolic curve, the roundness, like a hill, a path around a lake, the eyes circumscribing, embracing, surrounded and held by, and at the same time encircling, the return, after a journey, back to where you started, except that you have traveled, and all the texture of your trip, the uneven ground you have tread, the knowledge in the soles of your feet, has changed you, so that coming back, you are both different and more yourself. Though the false start would have come back on you too, had already shown itself as defeat and exhaustion, the flat lands of despair from which no escape seems possible, and in which you believe you just have to continue, spiritless and doomed to the same direction. But now you are released from that fate. You have seen the error. Like a punch-drunk boxer who plugs away at every shadow, you were stuck in argument. Defensive, aggressive, overzealous in your effort, lurching forward too fast, you failed to notice what was there. Just in the sentence before. Something beautiful still to be teased open. A motion more subtle than speed. And from that discovery you are able to detect a delicate trace of the erotic. The slight scent that can change an atmosphere by the smallest degree. But this, of course, is everything.

1997

THICKET – A PLAY IN ONE ACT

Two excerpts

from Scene II

To begin at the beginning
to begin
where the story starts
whenever that happens to be

When this first happened to me I don't know why but I began
to take notes. Maybe I hoped the whole event would make
sense in the end, or that at least it would take on a pleasing
form, like the score for a song, or a symphony.

Notation
narration
not strictly speaking
score
in no way
strictly speaking
can you follow
in no way
can you

Friend was crossing, she was crossing the, she was
run   run   was run   was crossing over
friend was crossing over the road   was run was cro
sing, cro   sing   over   run was crossed   was run was crossing.
Cycle, the cycle, she turned, she stepped, into the road, was
        run, motor, the motor, the

motor, was run, the cycle, stop the cycle, friend she was run,
              crossed over
in no way
can
I follow
(*pause*)
Can I
make a transition
shift, change
cover the distance
stretch over the space here
between what is not and
what is
between
thinness
and thickness

Thickness
a thick
thicket
a mass
a heft
what you hold
in your hand
lift
press, spread
wade through slide in
slip on, step on,
stuff,

you
yourself
thicket.

...

from Scene IV

...

And the words, the words after all, are irrelevant. They have
no meaning really. For instance take the word *death*. What is
it after all? It's only an abstract concept. Because death is al-
ways gradual. Even if it happens in one instant. The instant
expands. It's like taking an inch and cutting it in half. You still
have the other half. And you cut that in half and you still have
a last half don't you?
And you cut that in half,
and guess what
you have still another half,
and you can do that again,
and again,
and again
and again.
And so you see, there's really no death at all.
(*pause*)
Which is why it's better not to mention it.

Be careful what you say.
Why stir things up.
Don't say (*whisper or mouth*) death,
don't even think (*whisper*) dead, death, dying
Just think
heart beat, lung fill
life, alive,

(HEART BEAT   BREATH)
DON'T SAY, DON'T THINK
don't use that word *death*
don't say, don't think
don't say, don't think
don't say,

I want to tell you about DNA.
Shift your mind a bit,
don't think about D – – – –
focus on DNA.
Because it's amazing, isn't it.
All this information
the notation
the code
for who we are
embedded into
the little, these tiny…
what are they?
D N A.
I mean these are the letters
we use to indicate this… this stuff,
this thinnest possible part of
the thickness of us.
And if you think about it
DNA is like an alphabet,
like letters
spelling out
different forms of life.

So it makes sense to call
it DNA,
doesn't it?
And when you hear that sound
DNA
you think of it right away
this big
this little, this big
What do you think it is anyway?
DNA?
DNA.
In a funny kind of way
it sounds kind of pretty
don't you think?
But I mean
that's just arbitrary isn't it,
the sound of D
or N
or A.
Except, except
it's what your tongue
is made from
isn't it?
And your mouth
and your ears;
they're all in there
aren't they
in the
little

the little signs
the little notes
the big
what is it
anyway?
DNA.
DNA.
When you make that sound
DNA
it's kind of like the
DNA in your tongue, mouth, ears
is saying its name
DNA
singing its name
D-e-e-e-e-e-e-e-e
N-n-n-n-n-n-n
A-ye-ye-ye-ye-ye
and even if you write it
your hand, the ink
the paper, even the paper
is DNA
because the tree
came from DNA
and maybe the DNA in everything
sings, all the time
DNA   DNA
rolling down the river
singing out its name
like notes on a

big score
DNA
rolling down the river.
(*pause*)
When I was at summer camp
I saw trees
rolling down the
river on their way to
the paper mill
and I thought then
how do they get those
logs all dry and flat
and neat and ordered and
packaged and white
and ready to write on,
how do they do that?

And then when I was older, I met an artist who made paper
and it was very wet when she was making it and she put little
twigs in it or little bits of cloth. Things she would find when
she went on walks. I knew this because I used to walk with
her. And once we found the feathers of an owl, all arranged in
a circle where the owl had been before. Some hawk had proba-
bly eaten it. And she kept one of the feathers and that feather,
a piece of it, ended up in the paper she made. I want to tell
you about DNA. (*pause*)
But SOMETHING
Something is snapping inside me
Something has given way

I can't say
what has broken
I can't say
what's spinning loose
I'm just
a little bit
sailing.
Where am I going?
I wouldn't be able
to tell.
I seem to have lost
I seem not to have any say in the
matter. Something
is snapping
shuddering, shaking
yet I feel, I feel
a certain
shimmer. Why?
I can't say I know.
I've lost control.
Something is snapping
shuddering, shaking.
Something translucent
has come to stay
I can't say
what or where
I am going.
Something
has given way.

And I am
wondering
is this what it's like
like feathers?
Like feathers floating,
flying off in different directions, and landing
you never know where,
dispersing
and gradually, gradually
shedding their shape?
Is this what it's like a kind of
decomposition
rising up in the wind
even flying
spread, spread over everything
part of the air.
Gone, yes
terrifying, yes
but with a kind of sweetness,
is this what it's like
dissolving
to dust
becoming
nothing
not anything you can put into words
exactly but
it has a certain beat
limbs, skin
never so thin

foot deep in the density
washed with the
wide warp of it,
the warp and woof of it,
the end,
irretrievably gone,
is this what it's like?
The end of me
myself unwoven?

1992

PUBLIC OPINION

A small fraction said
they were wrong
had slipped on the slick
of surmise
and fallen,
were falling still
into a chasm of error,
They wished, they said,
the moment undone.

A somewhat larger segment,
eight percent of the whole,
were outraged that this question
be asked and
the matter might be moot
except a small portion of these,
one-sixteenth to be exact,
even threatened suit.

A kindred group but slightly larger,
nearly half of a third, lapsed
into silence, seemed stunned
when they were asked.
In this sort of case the surveyors,
trained to invite response,
would wait quietly and then whisper,
Do you have something to say?

But though soft on the lips
this query rebounded too when,
as if in a great mummer's
chorus, a larger mass
(over two-thirds),
shook their heads, gestured obscenely
threw up their hands and
muttered hardly decipherable phrases
that swept in hot waves
over the entire survey.

How to compute this response
is unclear. And
the results were
further obscured
as one-fifth laughed and
lightly juggled the
question, balancing it
on a proverbial tongue
making puns, turning
the question to symbol
and inside out
and finally on its head.

Another segment, eleven per-
cent in fact,
spoke grimly of blame, milling
the grooved texture of
wrong that slivers

and scrapes the skin of
reason.

The score of course
is more than one
hundred more than
what could be called whole
but this is so often the case.
Figures, bodies,
things, moments
in time drip over the edge of
charts, skew
the sum.

You can never be certain of public
opinion, and as your faith in
measurable quantity frays,
you will long to hold handfuls
to smell and swallow
mouthfuls of substance, to taste
that which does not exist in the proof,
a conclusion that finally
leaves you begging,
your teeth hitting air,
grinding against themselves
eating the last hope you had
for communion.

1996

TO THE FAR CORNERS
OF A FRACTURED WORLD

1

How would you
catch it
your hand on a pencil
tracing the
outlines?
A leg
entangled
with another leg
or heavy there
and hands
six or eight grasping,
holding like clamps

2

There would be some
fabric, pieces of a skirt
frayed rope, soiled, used and reused for
different purposes
hauling water, keeping the trunk of a
car closed and
this.

And there might also be
pieces of metal
making a chain
that encircles
goes around the body
around and around

3

Then, of course
you lose it
your painterly command
you cannot draw
you cannot imagine how.
You want to bring in
one of the old masters
one with the largest possible canvas
the one who painted creation
on the ceiling of consciousness
because the gaping space
your hands feel in the thick of
your inaction
is that wide.

4

Or perhaps
the portrait could show
a quiet moment
one that proceeded
what is happening,
peaceful in a
misleading sort of
way
like that portrait
from the seventeenth century showing
successful burghers
all in a row

all well dressed
some fully illuminated
standing forward, proud
others barely visible
a shadow crossing those faces.
And behind,
a deeper darkness.

5

But what you witness now
is not still
and your own eyes are
moving, moving
darting, looking up, away, shutting,
madly skipping
in the craziest dance,
dancing with what they see
all the way to the edge of
motion.

6

And what is this dance
our eyes follow?

The music
so strange
that high thin song
with the odd blue tone
and the cracking.

Is that how they sound
old bones?

7

Of course, gentlemen,
we hear you too
as you explain,
she is not your
grandmother

and this is not
your child either,
you tell us,
whose throat
just closed.

8

And who are you?
You are of course only human.
The curled paper
on which light has burned
the image of those you love
has grown damp with
heat
in your pocket.
You are tired.
Understandably so.
The tears you shed
twenty deaths back

are packed like ice
against the sore
stiffness that has
invaded you.
Just this morning
you woke alert
frightened at the soundlessness
of death, until
the smell of coffee
burned on the fire
reached you.
Then brushing the sleep from
your eyes,
you spent long moments carefully polishing
patiently threading the
necessary pieces of metal together
placing the eyepiece in line
with the proper instrument
so that all life
as you once knew it lay
composed
before that delicate juncture where
two stitch-thin crosshairs
meet.

9

Try to compose it,
it fails
the center
vanishes

the figures
suddenly
nowhere
in sight

or hiding under
scraps of buildings
the columns of a fallen bridge
anything hard will suffice
as shield
or
carapace.

Yet nothing stays
everything disperses
you cannot draw this
dust as it rises

and when
as the air clears
you are met
by the shock of a
body newly rent

your hands fly
off the page.

10

But of course
you can work from memory.
Were you the child who watched
as her sister was dragged beneath the house
by that gaggle of boys?
Were you followed
on the way home
yourself and pulled
flat? And if you escaped
still, so often and
quickly, quickly
you look back.

11

It is not so much a canvas that is needed
as an ocean
or a sky.
And you cannot paint this alone.
You could drown in this picture.
There are waves here
that can sink
the safest ships and you must
break
to hear them.

12

Consider then
the many perspectives
that are needed
or are
silent partners in this
arrangement, the viewpoint
of the lens at different ranges
upward to cosmic bodies perhaps exercising
their pull, inward to the cell, whose boundaries
are so transparent, down into the world of the
dead from whom all else is built,
or the viewpoint of the ones who make the lens,
who adjust the aperture
who make the metal casing,
ring after ring
which houses vision,
or those who make the other objects
bracelets, fences,
the moving parts of machines. Or
the viewpoint of those spinning
the thinnest threads
who weave our names into a cloth
that is laid upon the table
and the ones who sow
and collect what is there later
in the fields
and those who will finally make the bread
this vision is also needed.

13

Yet there is still another angle of sight
wholly impossible
what is unwitnessed
and must remain so
because all that we know
approaches
but does not enter.

Only those who have entered know
those who have been forced
to a knowledge that
severs knowing
into the smallest pieces
fragments flying into
the far corners of a fractured world.

14

So it remains to reassemble
whatever we can
on this holy or unholy day
on this day like any other
remembering
letting words fall into our mouths
like bits of a
shared meal
scanning the numerous texts,
rendering all the possible
readings,

scriptures various as
seeds, the many meanings
of this feast
the spilled wine of
our living.

15

And if given
what we see
every move
is riddled with pause
here in the hesitation
is where
the hand searching the page
first touches form,

though so much is missing
still it is here
you can begin to imagine
the arc of vision
bending home.

And though the severed
still shiver
inside
this circle
here is a place
we can meet

one to the other
the other to one.

1994

FAITH

Because of the numbers
blue tattoo
on his father's arm
or the doors
she was always taught
to lock
there was not
so much
belief as
wish and this
was thin, more
in body than
mind, though
the body would jump
of its own accord
at nothing
and the mind
compared this
life to perfect
lives and
suffered.
How nice it could be
but it was not meant
was how it all went
over and over.
But he was close
and she was near
even in the great
medium of fear

to the starting
charge of faith,
an entrance to
that other place of
no escape.

1989

RETRIEVE

Early in life
a child is carried
crying from
the theater.
Afterward
there will be films
she is forbidden
to see.
Later she sets her
teeth and staring
never even
shields her eyes,
though she knows
some sights are
etched before you
can look away.
Still by the time
her face
is lined
she'll learn
to turn
now and again
and find
another region, a
retrieve.

1989

HUNGER

*After photographs of refugees from famine in the
Sahel, taken by Sebastão Salgado, exhibited in
Paris, May, 1986.*

It is important to see this.

In the old texts
the world was made
after the image of justice

one photograph after another.

I stood there
taking notes

(I who hunger
for love).

In one of the images
someone tries to feed
a small boy. He is
mostly bone. A clear tube
enters his nose.
His eyes draw everything
into them.
In the moment the camera captures
the world
spins about his terror.

One could not reach out and touch him,
he was in another country,
only oneself
hand for a moment
shielding the eyes.

They say the world was created
by great love

yet for some reason
the letters were not written
in their proper order.

There was the breadth of it
the hunger of these people
who were not in the room.

I wrote in my notebook
before I can stop myself
I am shaken
it is the sight
of the child's buttocks
so deprived of flesh
they appear
like an empty bag, crumpled
over his legs.

Language is filled
with words for deprivation
images so familiar
it is hard to crack language open
into that other country
the country of being.

I have felt many kinds of longing.
And also despair.
Wanting what did not exist
what I believed I could not
continue without
the sweet taste of
bliss covering me
like a blanket.

In one photograph
thirsty boys
hear the first sounds of water
moving through a pipe.

I know what is possible
what exists in and out of language.
Why is it one wishes
to feel the dimensions of
being outside
the dimensions
of self?

They sit waiting
under the beautiful trees
the hungry
with light striking them
and the trees
their beauty.

Malgré le nombre considérable des morts
Despite the considerable number of deaths
les réfugiés gardent la dignité
the refugees hold onto dignity
et le respect des rites funéraires.
they practice burial rites.

Under this photograph I read
there is not enough wood
for coffins
so the bodies are wrapped
in the sacks
that have been used
to bring food.

Somewhere else it is written that
the love of creation
is a brilliantly shining light
and that it is the nature
of good to do good.

Behind these images
are many histories.
A long story traces
the beginning of hunger
past famine, past drought
to moments of blindness, places
where the full dimension
of being

was not known
and this led
to this image:
a small girl's body
webbed and spiny like an insect
hung in a scale,
this body
on which the light falls
as evenly
as any other,
the light
on this body
taken up by my eyes.

Where we see no image of justice
the word *injustice* reminds us of what we want.

Inside, this word
makes circles like the
hungry who cannot
stop seeking, who stumble
over mountains, through deserts.
Inside me this word
is like a lover
seeking the dimensions
of love.

References to the old texts allude to the thought of Menahem Nahum of Chernobyl, found in *Upright Practices, the Light of the Eyes,* translated by Arthur Green (New York: Paulist Press, 1982). Menahem Nahum was a Hasidic rabbi who was renowned for his teachings in the eighteenth century. The nuclear power plant that exploded in Chernobyl is built over the ruins of a Hasidic temple.

1986

✹✹✹

Now I write them down
these words that leap through me
as the order I expected today
sits like an admonishing aunt,
neglected.
Meanwhile outside the windows
another day goes on without me.
Wild winds, torrents of rain play
that wind chime my mother gave me.
So many of the pieces have blown away.
My mother, slow, ill, far
away, sits through her day.
Clock, dishes, letters, yes, yes
I feel all this, and a sudden
wish to slap the wall,
to slap it, keeping time.

1986

✭✭✭

I went very far away from life
with its torpor. I was out there
in the ethereal air
the cold rush against my face
was exciting
and even more
there was a kind of star that broke
my heart and made it wide
as space itself.
Now I have fallen again
and I rush arms open like a lover
or prodigal daughter.
Streets, gleam of pavement after rain,
my very human thoughts, my very human wants,
those old songs just now I am writing again
I love you, I love you again.

1985

SALLY

Just like you
to be fast at death

your quick eye
the wit

fast under the
least false move

you were true
as a good note

and tough in a
dazzling way

like you had
already found the mark

and deciding to stay
wanted to see

the rest of us
flounder.

We'd come to sit in your kitchen
soaking up fear with laughter.

I don't like that
you're dead, I'd say

Take the bread,
you'd answer,

and finish it off
you don't know what comes after.

1994

MIRACLE

It all happened on the water
Jesus' walking
the fishermen watching
from their boats.
When they picked up their nets
they half expected
a miraculous catch
but it was as ordinary
as the rest of the day.
Only some of them understood.
This is how it always is
with a vision.
Jesus walked on the water
only once.
This wasn't science.
What was it the fishermen were
supposed to see?
A man moving over the surface
of the sea as if it were
some other substance like ground.
Was this all there was?
Picture yourself
you are out there on the water
you look at that horizon.
You are so used to seeing that part
of the sky it's become
part of your eyes.
Then you blink, staring
you turn to shake your companion.

This was not what you expected to see.
Not even what you wished for.
What difference does it make
a man walking on the water?
But even so the day
going on as it usually does
is cut with a certain clarity
and you, you feel an inexplicable
happiness, the water
beneath you, the
bright air above.

1985

SEVEN NIGHTS

Seven nights.
We are already so well
into the miracle
it would be heresy to think
there will not be just
one more day.
But shouldn't you be
grateful for this: seven.
What is it that makes the number eight
so sacred?
Just this, it is a kind of language
sacredness speaks.
(She will use any form.)
Don't close your heart.
Don't think these meager potatoes
this little bit of oil
is all there is.
Such wretchedness is a way
of thinking.
The number eight rests on your lips.
It has become much more than a dream.
You know it as a feeling now, even familiar,
eight, you say to yourself,
aware you know now what all along
has been known, must
have been known somewhere, by someone,
eight days, and the dwelling place
of sacredness grows large inside you.

1985

COPERNICUS:
A TWENTIETH-CENTURY JOURNAL

1

Small worries, tasks and taxes, how to pay.

Beautiful day
a day for
intense
knowledge.

Earth calm now
after the quake
bridge broken
and death

the rocking
like a boat at sea
lost in immense waves
or the waters of the mind

uncertain
shaken
pulled from one
pole to the other,

natural order,
and the old, familiar culture.
Birds still here
but not such variety.

Bridge broken
but you can
fly the continent
before the sun sets

red leaves on the
East Coast
still trembling.

2

*So many compromises to get through a day. Driving
just a mile to pick up supplies. Had I been walking I
would have seen the sky it was so extraordinary.*

As the space
gets smaller one
wants to bring into it
St. Catherine laying herself
across the steps of that
church behind the
great square in
Siena and the eyes in
the mirror of Velázquez,
to draw in phrases of
Schubert and the rooms
in upper Manhattan
where you listened
to the old recording,
to save Aphrodite

or Apollo
to include
the delicate observations
of constellations
though you never quite grasp
the precision,
and a certain inflection
of the aleph
spoken in Kraków before
the war, the look of ecstatic
faces lost in thought, the
interior moment E.D. caught,
in her curious way, the butterfly
wings of a rare
species, exquisite
pages from the journal
circa 1700
anonymous
they thought the world
was
ending, or the cold
streets of London, last
century, dark
carriages, the rain
we don't care where
we are going
it is just the smell
of the air
fresh and wet

someone burning
pine, the wheel creaks
on the paving stones.

3

To love the world as we find it, body aging. And
mingled with the sense of loss, a softening.

To love this world,
being poised with
such perfection
in the fulcrum
of cognition
to live on Earth
and see stars.

Many old systems
dismantling.

Yellowing
onions
turning liquid
in the bag and

secretly
I love

what the earth promises
rare fermentation

weeks in the dark
newspaper spread
around the bed

smell of ripening
coffee.

4

The force of sensation stronger with age. And
feelings too complex to name.

Ass like two
smooth river
stones
breast and belly
of course
like hills
turning soft yellow
in the summer sun
on the curving
coast of California,
place in the cove
where oysters grow
bivalves, smell of sea
slippery in the mouth.

5

Mind moving slowly, as through a vast library filled
with hours, days, years.

And being
slow and swift
at once
you are both
hare
and tortoise,

hand reading the
shell, exaltation
of palm

intelligence of the smallest
bone making the web
from thumb to hand

able to measure
an ancient crater
on the dry airless moon

or small movements
of the tongue
speaking of 3.8 billion years
of living cells

broken by
PCB
floating in the deep sea

poison alphabet
spelled out in
generations
parody of procreation

the wonders
they spoke of
finding the new world
just as dreamed

whale oil
lubricating the
missiles which
land back
in the sea

Dürer choosing
just the right
brush for the
rabbit's fur.

Song of blessing.
Taste of wine,

what was the word for it?
Sound of the
flavor
sweet.

6

The longing, fiercer now, for all of it to continue
past my own existence.

What you might want
symbolic
after you're
gone

yet
breath
(mouth, ear, eye, skin)
as true as any
vision.

        And beneath the question
        regarding the properties
        of the universe
        which are embedded like
        jewels
        in your belly and
        will shine
        the length of your spine
        and in your hands

argument of the trees
argument of the stones
disquisition of gravity

treatise of the
wingspan

> you are also asking
> if the one who clings to
> ordinary reality
> with its earthly
> jealousy
> can be loved.

7

*Discovery this year. Elements needed for life found
on another planet. And for life to continue here?*

Come down from the
ancestor
meteor

> and searching now for
> life in space
> airwaves strategically
> scattered
> *Tell us something*
> *about ourselves.*
> *When you look*
> *in this direction,*
> *Who do you see?*

Earth from that distance
just one speck
mystery of placement,

      the desire
      to stay up all night
      smoking and drinking
      when the body
      does not wish it.

Asking the ocean
for forgiveness

      the infinite resonance of
      each alteration.

At the edge of
recognition
how Copernicus
stood
in this air

just thick enough to breathe
and thin enough to see

how the story
made its way
into being

and the earth shakes
in its own creation.

Beautiful universe
and the green
visitation.

1990–1997

GREAT AS YOU ARE

Be like a bear in the forest of yourself.
Even sleeping you are powerful in your breath.
Every hair has life
and standing, as you do, swaying
from one foot to the other
all the forest stands with you.
Each minute sound, one after another,
is distinct in your ears. Here
in the blur of mixed sensations, you can
feel the crisp outline of being, particulate.
Great as you are, huge as you are and
growling like the deepest drum,
the continual vibration that makes music
what it is,
not some light stone skipped on the surface of things,
you travel below
sounding the depths where only the dauntless go.
Be like the bear and
do not forget
how you rounded your
massive shape over the just ripened
berry which burst
in your mouth that moment
how you rolled in
the wet grass, cool and silvery, mingling
with your sensate skin,
how you shut
your eyes and swam far and farther
still, starlight

shaping itself to your body,
starship rocking the grand, slow waves
under the white trees, in the
snowy night.

1989

SPIDER

You are moving very slowly
across the ceiling.
How is it you know
where to move?
Your movements seem like
indecision, even the
confusion of the lost.
Where is it you
want to be?
Where will you
find comfort,
make your home
or do you
already have one?
Or is the white ceiling
another sort of country
for you
not one of resolve
but a pool
of blankness
the place where you
unravel your being
a web fusing with
that other web
there in the expanse.
Keep your mind open, I tell
myself as I glance away
travel a bit farther
with the spider

but now, turning back
I see you have disappeared
made your journey hidden
or even stopped
perhaps to crowd yourself
with darkness
and the closeness of space.
What is it like there
where you live and work
and make
a life?
I want to know and
have you taken
that big being
back with you
into the storehouse
the cradle,
the bedding ground
of grace?

1989

THE WHALES

They are like boulders
or plinths, strange
petrified shapes
signaling caves
beneath our feet
neolithic but asleep,
riddles of weight
they float
deep in the sea
vertically
erect with sex
and dream.

The whales
(full of sperm and oil)
awake will
eat whole schools
yellow and blue
striped, silver,
spotted blue,
arctic and warm, the widest
range of concept
swims into the maw
becomes
gray flesh
in the gullet.

And we
who eat with our eyes

wait for the arc,
dark waves
above the water
like so many fleeting
thoughts
here and gone in an instant
moments of thrill
that will sink
back to the liquid
place, the current
beneath the surface
where even now
we seek
the signs.

1996

DEATH HOLDS A CHILD

FOR JODIE

Death holds a child
as she is held
in a living woman's
mind. The world
is shattered and
rewoven in her
thought.
A blanket wrapped
around the earth
is made of glass.
Memory passes
through here easily
like light.
Splintering is certain.
Nothing ever stops
the loss, the constant
turnabout,
the green that always
comes again,
with hard cries of joy
fierce and pure as grief.
Each life, she knows,
immeasurably beautiful
and brief.

1997

THE PRESERVER

It was this that
the preserver knew
putting her hands
where the hands
of the others had been
that the inner state
begetting the old
images she touched
would be hers too
as she worked.
Who we are
is not simple.
She is for a moment
who *they* were
the masters.
Burned to our finest points
are we not
crystals of the same element?
But how differently
the element configures
in each
image or line, stroke of brush or
press of paper.
You can see this knowledge
in her laugh, the one caught
in the lens just
before it broke open,
leaving her in
emptiness

where even now
small waves begin
to form.

1990

ARCHIVE

The shape of abuse
is round with repetition.
What has been done to you
you will do.
And failing to see
you will be
not only two
faced at the gaming table
but blank
and vaguely absent
at the feast.

Here is my part.
I cannot forgive
and fixing my attention backward
repeat in speech
all that you fail to know,
knowing speech was the
bludgeon used on me
in childhood which I use
in my effort to be free.

Freedom of course eludes
the attempt. Still, just
on the other side of the circle
is the embrace
of a quieter knowledge,
unbound, unbattered,
coextensive with space

which surrounds our sad
cramped history with
archives of grief
and the impenetrable
mystery of grace.

1997

WINDOW

Look at how it happens
you are standing at the
newly painted window
and you see the clouds
as they come your way
blanketing the hill, just as
fog massing at the
edge of the water
starts to rise.
You see what
will come and pass
and come again.

1996

HOLY BODY

Late night fog
glows in the bay
like a holy body.
Morning slant
restores the trees
chalk white city
glass blue water.
By evening flushed
and spent
you grow dark again.
Mysterious and
constant lover.

1996

WINTER

This winter sickness
took hold of me
but I was ready
to be held
and fell willingly
into solitude and
dream.

In my mind
a numbing snow
covered hot
causality
and I began to wonder
at all my years.

Weariness is not a lesson
but it leavens
want.
There would perhaps
be other lives
to live
but reaching
into the warren where
soft creatures hide
my hand gestures
kindly,
Don't be afraid.
It's just you and I here

in the dark.
Nothing matters
but this.

1997

HOME

Either
I am dying
or I am not.
Perhaps there are
small animals
under the house
mouse, raccoon, rat,
though none of us
can find
a trace.
And late
a lone plane
makes a
straining sound
low over the trees
though only I
am awake.
Moments of quiet
are absolute
with depths
like the depths
of small pools
high in the mountains.
Everyone has the flu
rising and coughing
taking this or that
for the rasp.
Behind the blind
light still burns

at the edge of the bay.
Someone drives
over the bridge.
Home is
in every direction.

1997

CELEBRATION

FOR GEORGIA

This is your season,
incipient, working the ground for
and giving the first
signs of spring so shockingly
tender.
That split-second
flutter of knowing visible
in your eyes as
you see the invisible nuance
of soul, how birth is
everywhere, under and
inward, at the tip
of the tongue and
trailing the word
as it breaks past
any meaning
you would call reason.

This is your time;
flowering plum, quince and tulip,
mustard bright under the tree
are with you now, sweet
and tart as wit,
opening petal by petal like
blossoms of laughter but quick
coming back to the bud
of witness
the echoing rhyme.

This is the place
in the motion, that new edge of green
soft and sharply
real, touching the
hand that receives
everything. Nothing
left out of creation,

even misery and
grief bending
to stroke the skin of causation
to find the mysterious grain
the place inside the place.
Celebration.

1997

GRANDDAUGHTER

Lovely Sophie fresh
from the womb
breast, chest
shoulder, belly
this is your room.
All of us dance
happy around you.
And as you sleep
is that a dream
or just digestion
crossing your face?
Or perhaps
the sensation
of being new
which has entered us too
having prepared and counted
and gotten what we wanted
we're reeling with shock
at the palpable pureness
the disequilibrium of
loving you.

1997

NATIVE TO CALIFORNIA

My mother who
was smile
who was motion
wit
my mother who was welcome
turning in the glance
and laughter
now
ash.

My mother
one of the dead
her ashes
among the trees

live oak and pine
needles underfoot
native to California
as she was
born on the coast.
Long Beach
seaweed skirt
in the picture
aged five
heart shaped face
like my daughter

who was there
among us

laying her down
under the
lowest branches

the way the dead
used to be laid in trees
or sent out on the water
in the belly of a trunk
hollowed out and prone
like cargo.

In her last
hours they moved her
to the other side
of the building
and from there
she could see
a plum tree
past its bloom and bearing
but still
with the wine-dark leaves.

Afterward
in the bed
her body so small
hardly showing
under the sheet.

The necessity of trees
not for breath alone
or at least
one dimension of breath
the slow sigh
of the rib cage
blood quickening
wind in the nostrils.

How in earlier times
whole forests were downed
as timber for
the King's Palace
or so it is written

but something was lost
in the displacement

all that was left was dry
a wasteland
called wilderness.

Mother white
light in the hand.

I stood
with her
though she had left
late summer evening

as the light left the sky
the heat of my childhood
suffering gone.

Consider the way
the canoe is cut
from one great trunk
huge tree I saw
uprooted
once after a storm
branches as if sinking
into the wet
ground
stern and
hull
leaves, flowers carved
into the prow.

The same craft
every time and yet
with small differences
the force of meeting
in the making.

No, we did not accomplish
our love easily
The old photograph
dusty, with the smell
of medicine,

shows me, the length of
her arm,
a bundle she held
lightly and away.

She was so good with her hands
but someone else
taught me to draw.

Stern teacher
hair drum tight
and me just eleven
starting to bleed
and living in my
grandmother's
house.
She led us
outside
where the oaks
shadowed the school
and taught us all
boys and girls
to see how a trunk
rises from roots
how the branches continue,
lean like arms, how the leaves
spring from twigs
and the symmetry,
she taught us to look

and to follow the lines
pencil over paper.

Mother
there you were
are in my mind now
in the yellow kitchen
the margarine melting
in the cupboard
glasses in the sink
with decals
they gave us free
the year I came back
to you
our view out the window
over the sink
of the neighbor's weeds
and their old wrecked trailer.

The dinner trays all
finished, shiny aluminum
needing no washing
disposable
and what dishes are left
I wash
easily.

You hating the
discipline your

mother gave too
much
give me a used
desk, crude and
heavy but
wood.

One day the desk will
be yours
the drawers filled
with yellowing papers
and here
with all your things,
the flat
continuing pavement,
the roads and quick low
buildings
all around,
you will seem
almost exiled

except for that one
frail branch
we planted in the back.
Despite your
disbelief it
grew and gave you
fruit.

You with your dreams
of voyages.

Did you see
the cypress
pine
yew making a bell shape
did you taste
the laurel
have any knowledge
of the
needle-like rosemary
its slight sting on the
tongue
did you understand
the hesitating sweetness
of fennel
or glimpse
from the side
that wavering shade
of the plane tree
or the bald and then flowering
fist of the
sycamore
the silver light
of the olive.
No.
But it was you
your half-wise

wish
that made its way through
thick time
and brought me
to see.

Though you could
not pronounce the words
you knew them
by sight
arbre forêt feuille
dictionary in your lap,
a way to be
beyond and yet stay
a path of leaves
and pages

the foreign tongue
new to you but
ancient
Montaigne, Sévigné
rooted
tree forest leaf
in the journey back.

Ma mère, my
mother
making
another music

here in this
        cup
of words
the cupola
being
a circle
where you
who are nowhere
appear.

Searching for just the right
souvenir
to bring you
the mind strange in its
navigation
of grief
hand hovering over that
beautiful book
Pierre Loti
the traveler
his name raised
on the cover
hovering and hearing
impossible now
too late.

Color of sky
blue
ciel bleu

yellow
soleil jaune
or golden sun
shining
as you grew
thin
as shaved bark
sitting up
straight as timber
eyes wide in your face
and white with want
at the very edge of
your time
to give
the pearls,
the rings.

You will not understand
until it is past
the one who bore you
and was born herself
shall be born back
again to the
secret substance

the source
to be born
legs wide
the nourishing blood
spilling

and me,
my child,
my child's
child
a slippery mass
mouth wide as legs
and sounding.

And so at midday
we circled you
your two daughters
your granddaughter
while you opened the box
for the exchange
life and now this
glittering in our hands.

Then tired
you sank back
eyes fading
into the light
of the television
camera circling in air
to capture this image
a man on the ground
being beaten.
We speak of it but
for you
this is all over.

And the stories you tell
are told lightly
why you were afraid of flying
how the ring you gave me
was given and then sold
and then returned.
How Grandpa's mother
Sarah the one who
painted roses
put it on your finger
and how after the divorce
hard up for cash
you sold it to Grandma
who was
tight with money
we all knew it
no one even had to say it now
and how when Grandma died
you got the ring again
and now that it's mine
we are
laughing together
at the roundness
the conclusion of the
form.

How do I know
what she felt
back then?

Or if she roamed the rooms
looking to leave
because this was so much
earlier and I was
little,
but I know how she
looked
can find it in my
mind's eye
picture-frame neckline
scalloped borders
brown and white
and the shoulder pads
and thin brows
and bright red lips.

And I remember the sound
of the radio
pressed to a
Gothic arch
or the singles
the grooves
Art Tatum, the notes
dropped so elegantly
down, the pauses
throwing you
just a bit off
balance

swing.
I remember
the mischievous
smile, the
shy charm, head
cocked
Ain't Misbehavin'
along with the
eyes that began
to lose their focus.

After she died
I glimpsed
a woman her age
on a country road
walking
and I imagined

the pain of
other lives
in that music
what could have been
or was just
out of reach
all those fires
extinguished.

Recalling
the drum hewn from

a single piece of
wood,
violin
body of piano
keys and hammers
resonance of trees

and how in all the
ceremonies
you will touch
the laurel wreath, the
sprig of Daphne,
lodgepole, or
olive branch
as part of the
dance.

What was stripped
away
not only in the hills
where they mined
coal, gold, uranium,
timber
but in the cities
where the coal was burned
where the gold was spent
where other ruins were made
of body and
spirit.

Glad now
to relinquish
every trace of
bitter
history.

All that is necessary
in the intricate chemistry
(flames
in the life
of the Bishop
pine)

I hear her
inwardly
saying
keep the

seed
it will
burst open
in its own time.

(Think of
                Ashtoreth
fruitful, nourishing
earth, female deity
cinder or remnant
of star

asherah sacred trees
or *Bodhi*
tree of wisdom,
tree of life
the jaguar on San Blas
who stands in saltwater
the umbilical cord
the family tree.)

Mother
I can see you here
like the woman I glimpsed
at the side of the road
her body confident
rough like the
the country she inhabits,
hair like your hair,
the color of leaves,
aging

while the highways
and malls
and boxlike houses
are slowly overgrown and
erode,
the truth of time
finally ours.

The circle of soft
pain that settles now
around every thought of her

You who were so beautiful
as beautiful as water
black and splashed with
sunlight

you were swimming
in the photograph
we found

mother
light
ash in my hand.

You who were
root like Daphne
and have also been
taken
I lean
into the curve
of the past
for the scent of you.

1992–1998

ABOUT THE AUTHOR

A critically acclaimed and respected feminist writer, poet, essayist, lecturer, teacher, playwright, and filmmaker, Susan Griffin is the author of more than twenty books including *A Chorus of Stones: The Private Life of War; The Eros of Everyday Life: Essays on Ecology, Gender, and Society; Woman and Nature* and *Pornography and Silence,* as well as several collections of poetry, including *Like the Iris of an Eye* and *Unremembered Country.* The recipient of numerous grants and awards, Griffin lives in the hills of Berkeley, California.

The typeface is Chaparral, designed by Carol Twombly for Adobe. Chaparral combines elements of the slab serif designs of the 19th century with the lively letterforms of the Renaissance. In 1994, Carol Twombly became the first woman to receive the Association Typographique Internationale Charles Peignot Award for outstanding contributions to type design. Book design and composition by Valerie Brewster, Scribe Typography. Front cover design by John D. Berry. Printed on Glatfelter Author's Text, an archival quality paper (acid-free, 85% recycled, 10% post-consumer stock). Printing and binding by McNaughton & Gunn.

↯↯↯